"Oh Rick!"

It was a half sob, catching in her throat. Her breathing was ragged.

He caught her by the shoulders and held her slightly away from him. His eyes were hot, smoldering with a dark fire. "You're supposed to say, 'You shouldn't have kissed me like that,'" he whispered fiercely.

Michelle shook her head. She felt the sudden flame of humiliation burn in her cheeks.

"All right. I'll say it for you. I no longer have the right to do that. I guess I forgot for a moment that this isn't yesterday. But old habits die hard, my love. . . ."

RUTH LANGAN

describes herself as a full-time mother and part-time writer. Happily married to her childhood sweetheart, her busy household consists of five children, including a set of twins. Tiny and blond, she skiis, bowls, golfs and jogs several miles a day.

Dear Reader:

Silhouette Books is pleased to announce the creation of a new line of contemporary romances—*Silhouette Special Editions*. Each month we'll bring you six new love stories written by the best of today's authors— Janet Dailey, Brooke Hastings, Laura Hardy, Sondra Stanford, Linda Shaw, Patti Beckman, and many others.

Silhouette Special Editions are written with American women in mind; they are for readers who want more: more story, more details and descriptions, more realism, and more *romance*. *Special Editions* are longer than most contemporary romances allowing for a closer look at the relationship between hero and heroine with emphasis on heightened romantic tension and greater sensuous and sensual detail. If you want more from a romance, be sure to look for *Silhouette Special Editions* on sale this February wherever you buy books.

We welcome any suggestions or comments, and I invite you to write us at the address below.

Karen Solem
Editor-in-Chief
Silhouette Books
P.O. Box 769
New York, N. Y. 10019

RUTH LANGAN
Just Like Yesterday

Silhouette *Romance*

Published by Silhouette Books New York

America's Publisher of Contemporary Romance

SILHOUETTE BOOKS, a Simon & Schuster Division of
GULF & WESTERN CORPORATION
1230 Avenue of the Americas, New York, N.Y. 10020

Distributed by Pocket Books

ISBN: 0-671-57121-4

First Silhouette Books printing December, 1981

10 9 8 7 6 5 4 3 2 1

Chapter One

"Are you still anxious about this trip?"

The sound of the deep voice brought Michelle out of her reverie. She glanced at the man beside her who was driving expertly.

"I told you not to get yourself all worked up over this. It'll work out fine, you'll see." His eyes crinkled as he grinned at her. "We'd better stop to eat pretty soon. After nearly five hours of driving, I'm really stiff." Then, winking, he added, "You know what they say. It's tough getting old."

At this, they both burst out laughing. It had become the standard office joke. Two months ago, when handsome Jim Bannon celebrated his fiftieth birthday, the entire office staff had begun teasing him about getting old. The joke, of course, was that

Jim Bannon was lean and muscular, often jogging five or six miles each day. He dressed in the latest modern fashion, and had recently bought a snobbish sports car, which added to his youthful, vigorous image. When he joined a car club, which met twice a month to discuss their latest models and to drive in local rallies, the teasing had intensified. It was hinted by several of the men in the office that Jim was trying desperately to recapture his youth.

Glancing out the window, Michelle said, "There should be a fork in the road about a mile or so up there. If you keep to the left, there's a great little tavern—or there used to be," she quickly amended. It had been such a long time since she last drove on this highway that she wasn't sure if any of the old landmarks were still here.

Since they were on a rather deserted stretch of highway, Jim pressed down on the accelerator and thrilled to the surge of power under the hood of the car. Michelle smiled to herself. She had no fear of the speed. In fact, she thought it would be fun to drive Jim's car. She would have preferred being the driver to being a passenger.

She turned her head and watched as Jim expertly handled the turns. His suit jacket was tossed casually across the seat behind them. He had loosened his tie and rolled back the cuffs of his starched ivory shirt. His nearly white hair was thick and wind tossed. He was darkly tanned from a summer on the golf course, and it contrasted sharply with brilliant blue eyes that crinkled when he smiled. He had, Michelle thought, a typically "smiling Irish" look about him, which made people respond warmly to him. Jim's wife had died nearly three years ago. Michelle knew that his heavy work schedule, and his recent involvement in fitness and sports cars were his way of combating the loneliness.

Leaning back, Michelle drank in the beauty of the countryside. When she and Jim had left Detroit this October morning, the leaden skies had opened up in a torrent of rain, but here in northern Michigan the sun was shining and the pavement was dry. Though many of the trees were already bare, standing like gaunt, gnarled derelicts, many more still clung stubbornly to their brilliant red and gold leaves, which the wind snatched and scattered in fiery showers.

When they arrived at the fork in the road, Jim slowed the car and looked questioningly at Michelle. She nodded, and he turned left. In a short while, they drove up to an old fashioned, white frame house, which had been converted to a tavern. Inside, gauze curtains had been drawn against the bright sunlight, creating a dim, hazy glow. Family portraits of bearded men and corseted, prim women lined the walls of yellowed wallpaper. The antique furniture was set about without any apparent eye for style.

As Michelle made her way to the ladies' room, Jim walked up to the small bar and ordered a drink. When Michelle joined him a few minutes later, he looked up smiling.

"Would you like a drink?" he asked.

"Yes. White wine, please," she said.

Turning to the woman behind the bar, she asked,

"Do they still serve those sandwiches made with homemade bread?"

The woman nodded, and Michelle and Jim ordered lunch. When the woman returned, the sandwiches were as delicious as they looked. They were made with home-baked bread, thick and crusty, piled high with thin slices of rare roast beef.

While they ate, Michelle and Jim talked companionably. They were completely comfortable with each other.

Twenty-four-year-old Michelle Miller Scott worked for Jim at Forest Corporation. She had started with the company when old Joseph Forest was the owner. When his health began deteriorating, Michelle had absorbed most of the day-to-day routine. In grateful appreciation, Joe had created the title Assistant to the President, just for her. When he died, Jim Bannon had been named to replace him. If he had chosen to, Jim could have eliminated Michelle's title and position.

Instead, he had worked closely with her, encouraging her. They worked well together. She, the widow who had never really known the joys of marriage. He, the widower after nearly thirty contented years with his wife. Jim was relaxed and cheerful. Michelle was volatile and aggressive. Together they had become a formidable team.

"Are you still worried about this weekend?" he asked.

She nodded. "Just a little. Oh, I'll admit it's really great to have a weekend in the country at company expense. It's been such a long time since I've been out of the city." She sighed. "And it's a beautiful time of the year to be in the north country. But, honestly Jim, I'll be so relieved to get the first meeting over with. I think after I've had a chance to meet Mico's board of directors and answer their questions, I'll probably relax and enjoy myself."

He patted her hand, and grinned. "Trust me, Michelle. When they see how informed you are about the operations of our company, you'll have them eating out of your hand."

Grimacing, she remarked, "I hope you're right."

They left the tavern feeling refreshed and walked o the car. Settling themselves comfortably, they urried on toward their destination.

Cresting a hill, they sped past a deserted country church. Alongside it stood a cemetery, surrounded by a partially collapsed fence of iron posts. Tombstones lay in disarray among the weeds and brick and mortar from a crumbled wall.

Michelle absently twisted the delicate gold band on the third finger of her left hand. Her thoughts turned to David Scott. Dear David!

She thought of the simple grave marker, on a wind-swept hill at Holy Cross. The engraved words were etched in her mind. "David Scott. Age 26. Beloved husband of Michelle."

Husband! Such a bizarre title, she thought. She had loved only one man in her life. When he left her, her world fell apart. While she had put the pieces of her life together, David had been there for her, quietly offering his friendship when she had needed it. Later, when his world crumbled around him, during the long days of his illness, Michelle had been a loyal friend to David as well. Their friendship had never blossomed into love. But when David asked Michelle to marry him, knowing that their marriage would never be consummated, facing the knowledge that he would never again leave his hospital bed, Michelle agreed.

Their wedding, performed in the small hospital room, had been quiet, somber. But if there was no laughter or gaiety, there were also no tears. Michelle gripped David's limp hand in her own strong one, and proudly repeated her vows. Her promise to love and cherish his memory was the only gift she could give him. It was all he wanted. And so, together they had spoken their vows, and Michelle had taken his name as her own.

Afterward, Michelle lingered, holding his hand, feeling the life ebb slowly from his frail body.

Few people knew her story. Michelle never spoke of it. And most of the employees who came into contact with her would have been stunned to know that this attractive young widow had never known the wondrous joys of lovemaking.

Most of the people who worked with her thought she had become aggressive in business in order to forget her loss. But earlier in her life, Michelle had learned to deal with painful losses. Her aggressive attack on the business world had begun long before she had ever met David Scott.

An hour later, as the car turned onto a narrow road leading to Harbor Springs, Michelle felt all the memories of her childhood flooding over her. Harbor Springs was the summer playground for the old, wealthy families of the Midwest. The "cottages" were actually large estates, with carefully tended lawns, tennis courts and swimming pools. Michelle had spent all her summers here until college. Then had come the scandal. She had not been back since.

Squaring her shoulders, Michelle stared out the windows as they drove slowly through the town. Her thick auburn hair, which fell to her shoulders in a soft pageboy style, reflected the late afternoon sun and seemed to dance with liquid fire. Her large blue-green eyes were fringed with long lashes, gold tipped in the sunlight. She was small, fine boned and much slimmer than when she had been in her teens.

.Packing for this weekend had required a lot of thought. Michelle wanted to create an efficient, businesslike effect without appearing too prim. For Jim Bannon's sake, she knew that the impressions she made on this trip were important. On an impulse, she had tossed an old pair of jeans and comfortable canvas shoes in her suitcase. Maybe she could slip away from everyone and ride a horse for an hour or two. Or perhaps she could rent a bicycle in town. She had been forced to live for so long now on crowded city streets, filled with traffic and crowds of people. It would be heavenly to just walk down a deserted country road.

Jim and Michelle both knew that their future could be decided this weekend. Their company, Forest Corporation, had been approached by a company called Mico Industries regarding a possible merger. Mico was vague about its operations, but was assumed to be part of a conglomerate. Michelle was certain that she would find out much more about them this weekend. When Mico first proposed the merger, Jim had recommended that they work directly with Michelle, to make the transition as comfortable as possible. Mico had then issued an invitation to Jim and Michelle to attend a weekend business meeting here at Harbor Springs. They would have an opportunity to meet with some of the Mico legal staff. If approved, Michelle would be assigned to act as liaison between Forest Corporation and Mico Industries.

Michelle tried to calm the butterflies in her stomach. This weekend meant so much to both of them. If the merger went smoothly, Jim Bannon would see his company expand and become financially secure. If Mico agreed to keep him on in a top management position, his future was safe.

As for Michelle, she had worked her way up slowly in Forest Corporation, doing any job assigned her. Nothing had seemed too difficult, as long as she kept inching her way up the company ranks.

Michelle's fondness for old Joe Forest had been genuine. To her, he had been a gentle, grandfatherly figure. Jim Bannon had not only filled Joe Forest's job, but he had seemed almost immediately to assume the same protective role toward Michelle. He valued her hard work and her opinion. He had hand-picked Michelle to coordinate this merger, and he trusted her completely to handle any problem which might arise. Jim Bannon had become her father, brother and friend.

Pressing her sweating palms together, Michelle vowed silently to work harder than she had ever worked in her life to bring about the merger as smoothly as possible.

As they passed the harbor, where only a few small craft bobbed near the dock, Michelle remembered the harbor as it had been during the tourist season when she was younger. Yachts, sailboats, cabin cruisers, all displaying the flags of their respective yacht and boat clubs, docked here. The summer had seemed like one continuous party. Each year, on the Fourth of July, the Harbor Springs yacht race was held. It was the highlight of the tourist season. Everyone for miles around lined the harbor to watch. Afterward, parties seemed to spring up everywhere to celebrate the festivities.

Driving past the Harbor House Hotel, Michelle noted that it was freshly painted. Although it was an old hotel, it was kept in immaculate condition. The overflow of wealthy guests in the town always stayed at the Harbor House. The owner, Henri LaRue, was a congenial host, who personally supervised the kitchen, and saw to it that only exceptional meals were served to his guests.

Seeing the rolling, spacious lawns, Michelle looked beyond them to the now-deserted mansions. She remembered their own home, The Oaks. Each year, in May, the servants would be dispatched to Harbor Springs to open the house and get it in living order for the summer. At the end of the summer season, the Millers would drive back to their home in Detroit, leaving Rose and Lon, the West Indian couple who had been with them since before Michelle was born, in charge of closing up their summer home. Michelle had never given much thought to the work that must have gone into maintaining their summer place. Now, staring at the vacant windows, she imagined how the insides of the houses would look. The furniture would be covered with sheets to keep out the dust. Ornate rugs would be rolled up and moved away, possibly to attics, for storage. Plastic sheeting would be secured over windows to prevent the frigid winter air from attacking the hand-worked wood railings and moldings. Priceless paintings and sculptures would be carefully packed for the return trip to their winter homes.

Michelle had never been in Harbor Springs in the off-season. It looked, to her, like a ghost town. Except for an occasional gardener putting the final touches on a fence or shrub, and one or two local residents out raking leaves, this part of the town seemed deserted. Bicycle racks in front of shops stood empty. The small ice cream shop was boarded up.

Michelle wondered if she would bother to go and see her old home, The Oaks, while she was in town. She hadn't seen it since that summer when she was eighteen. When it was time to sell it, she had asked Rose and Lon to pack up the furniture and valuables. A local agent arranged the sale. When it was time to sign the papers, the lawyer had brought them to her home for her mother's signature, since her mother by then was no longer able to make the trip to the lawyer's office. No, she thought, she wasn't sure she would want to see The Oaks. It would be just another ghost from her past.

Jim looked over at her. "You're awfully quiet. Does this bring back a lot of memories?"

She nodded, afraid to trust her voice at that moment.

Jim braked at a crossroads. Glancing at a road sign, he said, "I'm supposed to turn right at Harbor Road. Do you think I may have missed it?"

Michelle looked around. "No, Jim. I'm sure Harbor is up there a bit." She shrugged apologetically. "Sorry. I'm not sure. It's been awhile. But let's go a little further."

"Yes," he replied mechanically, as he turned his attention to the road. "Judging by the looks of this place, your family must have been loaded."

"For a while," she replied unenthusiastically. She didn't need to elaborate. Jim Bannon, like Joe Forest, had been made aware of Michelle's family history. She felt it necessary, if they were to work well together, to be completely honest about it. Both men had admired the way she had handled herself in the situation.

Loaded! An appropriate description. Funny. She never gave it much thought anymore. Her life had taken such turns. The life she once lived, the girl she had once been, were strangers to her now. What would her life be like today if things hadn't changed?

As a girl, Michelle hadn't been taught to do the simplest tasks around the house. She never made a bed, or hung up her clothes, or washed a dish. If she tried on a dozen dresses before dinner, tossing each reject into a heap on the bed, she would return later to find them neatly pressed and hung in orderly rows in her closet. It was all taken for granted.

And when it had all come crashing down around her one deceptively gentle August morning, it seemed unlikely that she could ever adapt to her strange situation. Her mother never accepted it. And her sister, Connie, had run. In fact, was running still.

Michelle had been forced to reach deep inside herself to find the resources to adjust and survive. No one would ever realize how terrifying it had been to learn that she had no one but herself to lean on. And that "self" was an untrained, naive girl. But she had found within herself the strengths needed to survive.

The effects of her early years were still recognizable. There was a casual elegance about her. The way she wore her clothes. The way she walked. And an arrogance. In the way she tossed her head. The way she fought for what she wanted, tempered now with an appreciation of the work done by others.

She considered that life she had once known to be like a dinosaur—extinct. If her financial situation suddenly improved by some miracle overnight, Michelle knew she could never go back to the way she had been. She had learned to depend on herself. And she liked it.

As they turned down a secluded road, she exclaimed, "The Winter Castle! It must be!"

Jim glanced at her. "You know where we're headed?" he asked.

"If I'm right, this company must have leased the old Winter Castle. It's at the end of this road. Wait 'til you see it, Jim. It's fabulous! It was always my favorite!"

As they drove, they passed a low stone wall, which followed the dips and curves of the land. At the end of the road huge rusted iron gates stood open. Beyond, amid overgrown gardens and rolling hills, stood a three-story stone mansion, resembling for all the world a castle from another time and place. A wide veranda encircled three sides of the house. Bare windows seemed to greet them like sightless eyes in a brooding specter.

Jim glanced at the slip of paper in his hand, then read the number on the gate. "This is it," he said. "Is it the one you thought it might be?"

She nodded, swallowing a lump in her throat.

As the car pulled up to the stone steps, a young man about Michelle's age came toward them. He was dressed in jeans and a cotton shirt, with the sleeves rolled up above his elbows. Smiling, he opened Michelle's door and offered his hand.

"Hello," he called. "You must be Mr. Bannon and Mrs. Scott."

Michelle smiled at him. He returned the smile and said, "I'm Mac. Anything you need while you're here, just call me."

"Hello, Mac," she said, smiling.

Jim came around the car and shook his hand. Taking the keys from Jim, Mac opened the trunk and lifted out their luggage. "Go ahead in, folks. The boss is inside."

Michelle and Jim climbed the steps and entered the front foyer. The hardwood floors were dull with age and neglect. The late afternoon sun slanted through the large windows, making a path of light across the floor. As they crossed the entrance, a door was opened, and Michelle found herself staring into a face from her past. The face of Erick McCord.

"Rick!" Her mouth formed his name, but her voice seemed lost. No sound escaped her. Michelle hoped she didn't look as shocked as she felt.

Rick's features seemed frozen in granite.

Jim Bannon appeared to be completely unaware of the impact of their meeting. He walked past her and offered his hand. Rick reacted immediately, with only his raised eyebrow indicating that he was puzzled.

As they shook hands, Jim said, "Hello, Mr. McCord. I'm Jim Bannon." Then, turning to Michelle, he added, "And this is my assistant, Mrs. Scott."

Rick now turned and took her hand. It had turned to ice. She was trying, but not quite succeeding, to look unruffled.

"I know—Mrs. Scott," he said evenly. "Although I had no idea that she was the assistant you mentioned during our telephone conversation, Jim."

Rick turned his attention fully to Michelle, and she thought that at any moment her legs would betray her and she would fall in a heap at his feet.

"How are you, Mike?" he asked.

She stiffened at his use of that name. Rick

McCord was the only one who had ever called her that.

Her heart hammering, she said, "Fine, thank you, Rick," as she firmly extracted her hand from his.

He stared at her a moment longer, his black eyes glinting angrily, then he stood aside to allow them to enter the room.

"I'm sure, after that long drive, you'd like a drink before you see your rooms." Rick spoke to Jim Bannon, completely ignoring Michelle.

"Sounds good," said Jim cheerfully. "I'll have Scotch. Michelle drinks wine. White."

Rick fixed their drinks and handed them over, allowing his glance to linger on Michelle's face as she reached for her glass. She stared at a spot on the carpet until she felt him turn back to Jim.

While the two men talked, she sat down and allowed herself to stare at the man she had once wanted more than anyone in the world, and then had prayed she might never have to see again.

How could this be! The most important weekend in her career, and it was to be decided by the one man who would take delight in destroying her.

Rick McCord hadn't changed too much in six years. His hair was still thick and dark, although he wore it a bit shorter than when she had last seen him. His dark eyes still glinted like pinpoints of steel. His features seemed harder, chiseled out of rock. Rick McCord had never been handsome. His chief attraction had always been a kind of magnetism. He was a compelling figure. Tall, over six feet, with massive shoulders. He was lean and trim. He still had that aura of vitality, as though he could outrun, outwork and outplay any other man.

As she sat openly staring at him, he turned and caught her eye. Immediately, she looked away. She couldn't bear having his eyes on her.

A short time later the door was opened, and Rick said, "Mac will show you to your rooms. I hope you don't mind a late dinner. I've asked my lawyer and several associates to join us."

"That's fine," said Jim, glancing at Michelle. "We stopped earlier for sandwiches."

"Good. Dinner at nine, then," Rick said, staring at Michelle.

She turned quickly and followed Mac up the broad, dusty stairs.

Michelle had been given a corner room, overlooking the back terraces and pool. Beyond, the lake glistened in the fading sunlight.

She stared around her. This room, she knew, had once belonged to Mr. Winter's granddaughter, Marla. Marla had been the talk of the town. When her parents had been killed in a tragic plane crash, the old man had brought her here to live with him. He had lavished her with all that money could by. He bought her a pony and had a stable built on the grounds. A pool was installed so that Marla wouldn't have to swim in the lake. Neighboring children were regularly invited in to play with her so she wouldn't feel lonely.

The bedroom had been fit for a queen, with

canopy bed, thick, luxurious carpeting, expensive paintings and sculptures. Over the bed hung a portrait of a young, smiling Marla Winter. Michelle studied the portrait. Marla had been a tall, lively girl, with long, golden curls and pale, blue eyes. Though thin, she could never have been described as delicate. Everything about Marla Winter was vibrant and alive. She had ridden her horse at breakneck speeds, jumping fences and ditches with great skill. When she grew older, her red sports car had been famous in this area. Marla handled it as she handled everything else—with wild abandon.

When Michelle had been a little girl, Marla was already an international beauty whose parties were the most lavish ever seen in these parts. Michelle used to walk down the darkened dirt road that led to the Winter Castle and stand outside the brick wall, watching the couples twirl past the great windows. The sound of music and laughter would drift out on the summer breeze. Those were the half-remembered magic years in Harbor Springs.

By the time Michelle was in high school, Marla had gone to Europe. Rumor had it that an Italian count was pursuing her across the Continent, determined to marry her. By then, her grandfather was an old man, consigned once again to living alone, while his beautiful granddaughter flitted around the world like a rare butterfly.

To Michelle, the house had always seemed to reflect the moods of those who lived here. Whenever Marla had been in residence, the house rocked with music and laughter and gaiety. Whenever Marla left, the house became somber and restless, waiting to be called back to life.

Michelle stared at the portrait above the bed. What had become of the beautiful, lively Marla? Had she found love forever after with her Italian count?

Michelle shivered suddenly. Though the room was comfortably warm, she felt chilled to the bone. Filling the tub with warm water, she stripped off her clothes. It would be good to wash away the dust of the long drive. She only wished she could wash away this entire trip as easily.

Michelle tried to relax in the sunken tub. She needed to be calm while she worked out in her mind the shock of seeing Rick again. She had been deliberately trying to avoid thinking of him since she came upstairs.

When Jim had first mentioned Mico Industries to her, she hadn't even thought to ask for names. After all, most corporations today were dozens, even hundreds of investors. She hadn't even remotely thought about Rick. But from things she had read in recent years, she knew that Rick wouldn't be content to just work for Mico Industries. He *was* Mico Industries.

Sooner or later, she would have to explain to Jim Bannon why she couldn't work with Rick on the merger. It was going to be a mess, she knew. She had brought all the papers, had spent weeks going over all the details. There was really no one else at the Forest Corporation who was as well informed as she was on this particular issue. Ironic, she thought grimly, that as informed as she had thought she was, she had never even bothered to know the name of the man she would be working with so closely. Why had his name never come up? Try as she did, Michelle couldn't remember a single instance when Jim had mentioned the name of the person they were meeting. As a matter of fact, Michelle had assumed they would meet a board of directors, and after their initial approval of her, they would assign some junior partner to be their liaison with her.

Michelle stepped from the tub and wrapped herself in a large plush bath sheet. Walking to the window, she again looked out beyond the terraces to the lake, now cast in evening shadows. It was unbelievable that she should meet Rick here in the Winter Castle. That summer, when she was eighteen, she and Rick had spun their daydreams around this very place. He was to be her knight in shining armor who would carry her off to this castle, where they would live happily ever after. They had both laughed about it, but later, in the dark shadows of the rose arbor, he had kissed her solemnly and repeated his promise. Her heart had nearly burst from happiness.

Angrily, Michelle walked to the dressing table and unpinned her long hair, brushing it vigorously. As she stared at her reflection in the mirror, she suddenly dropped the brush with a clatter and strode across the room to the bed.

All the work that had gone into this merger, all the anticipation she had felt this morning about this weekend in Harbor Springs, would be for nothing because of the man downstairs who could see clear through to her soul with his cold, steely eyes.

She dropped the towel and climbed naked under the coverlet. She needed to rest if she wished to make it through the long ordeal of dinner. But sleep wouldn't come. Instead, Michelle began remembering clearly all the stunning events of her eighteenth summer here at Harbor Springs.

Chapter Two

That May, Michelle had graduated from the exclusive convent school she had attended since first grade. She was eagerly looking forward to college in the fall. Her parents had enrolled her in a prestigious women's college, which shared a campus with a men's university. From the giggled whispers of some of her friends, she knew that her life in college would be a far cry from the regulated life she had known at the academy.

Michelle spent the early part of that summer in Harbor Springs getting reacquainted with old summer friends. There were occasional dances at the Yacht Club, and endless rounds of tennis and swimming. In the late evenings, Michelle and her friends sat around the darkened porches trying to look sophisticated by smoking cigarettes. Most of the boys in the crowd carried bottles of whiskey which they had sneaked from their parents' bar shelves. Michelle tried drinking a few times, but had discovered early that she simply couldn't stand the taste of whiskey. Even now, she enjoyed only an occasional glass of wine.

Rick McCord had not entered her life until that summer was half over. He arrived for the Fourth of July yacht races with a group of friends. Michelle's older sister, Connie, who would be a senior in college in the fall, came home filled with stories about Rick and his friends. Connie was hanging around with their sophisticated crowd and couldn't stop raving about Rick McCord.

Michelle would never forget the first time she met Rick.

It was a hazy, humid afternoon. Before leaving for lunch with friends, Mrs. Miller promised Michelle she could have the car for the day. Once they were alone, Connie launched into one of her typically ugly scenes.

"I don't care what Mother said, Missy. You're not getting the car today. I've already promised the girls I'd drive. We're going to the Anders' lodge. Some of the guys are having a party there, and I don't intend to miss it. Especially if Rick McCord is going to be there."

She wrenched the keys from Michelle's hands and hurried to the back door.

"Connie!" Michelle shouted. "You've had the car every day this week. Mom promised me."

Connie laughed as the screen door slammed.

Michelle rushed to the door and shrieked, "I'll tell Dad when he comes home, Connie! I mean it! This time I'll really tell him!"

Connie was still laughing as she backed the car out the driveway. The tires squealed as she drove off in a rush.

Michelle ran up the stairs two at a time and paced her bedroom floor.

"Blast!" She kicked the bed. The whole afternoon stretched out before her, with nothing to do. Without even glancing in the mirror, she pulled her hair back with a rubber band, and yanked on an old frayed pair of cut-off jeans over her bathing suit.

Michelle stormed out of the house and ran the two blocks to the stables. She mounted her favorite horse, Marble, and turned him toward the woods. Once on the trails, she let Marble have his head. After racing along the tree-shaded trails, she slowed her horse and turned him toward a deserted stretch of beach. She didn't want to run into any of her friends. She was still too furious with Connie to be sociable.

"This whole summer is turning into a stinking disaster, Marble, she murmured to the horse.

Most summers, she and her father had spent entire days in their boat, fishing, often saying nothing, just enjoying each other's company. Sometimes, they would sit up half the night, talking incessantly, sharing with each other all the private things they had kept bottled up until they were together. Michelle adored her father. And she knew that he had a special place in his heart for her, too.

Once he had told her, "Missy, you're very special to me. Don't ever forget that. I'm expecting great things from you. I love your mother and Connie very much. You know that. But, honey, you're my special girl.

This summer, her father was hardly ever here. He had flown in for only two weekends. The rest of the time, he was in Detroit and New York in a frenzy of work. Michelle hated being cooped up with her mother and Connie. She couldn't wait until the fall, when she would leave for college.

Lost in her own thoughts, Michelle walked her horse through the waves near the shore. Then, feeling hot and sticky from the ride, she slid from the horse's back and led him further into the water. The cold water felt good against her bare legs. She led the horse deeper, not caring where they were headed, when suddenly she heard a voice shouting.

"Hey! Watch it! There's a drop-off there!"

The horse stumbled and began swimming. Tugging on the reins, Michelle began shouting at the horse to turn back. He was dragging her with him, and her shorts were already soaked. Still clinging to the reins, she pulled furiously. She slipped and tumbled headlong into the lake, gulping water.

An arm like steel pulled her upright, and a warm, deep voice said, "Just let go the reins. Otherwise, he'll keep dragging you in deeper."

Giving up the reins, Michelle turned and looked into dark eyes, glinting with humor. His lips were quirked in a half-smile, as though he found this whole thing amusing.

"Dumb horse!" she muttered, trying to walk gracefully through the deep water.

As a wave washed over her, she stumbled and again fell into the deep. She came up sputtering and coughing. The band had pulled out of her hair, causing it to fan out in a wild tangle of fiery red-gold strands. Chuckling, he offered his hand, and she was aware of the power of his grip. He pulled her toward him as though she were a feather.

"I think I'd better hang onto you until I get you to shore," he said.

Walking slightly behind him, holding his hand, she watched in fascination as the muscles of his shoulders rippled under his wet T-shirt. As they approached shallow water, she realized that he wasn't wearing a bathing suit, and his cut-off jeans, like hers, were soaked. Near the shore, his shoes were lying in a jumble. He must have thrown them off quickly before going out to her.

When they reached the sandy shore, he sank down on the beach, and Michelle flopped down angrily beside him.

"That stupid horse!" she muttered.

"I thought he behaved just like a horse," he said, grinning at her.

Gritting her teeth, she said, "I guess I just wasn't thinking."

"I'd say you were doing some heavy thinking," he said, turning toward her. "You looked like your mind was a million miles away."

"I guess it was," she said, frowning at him. "I didn't even see you over here." She glanced down at his wet shorts. "I'm sorry you got all wet. Do you have a towel or anything?"

He shrugged. "Nope. I hadn't planned to go in swimming in these," he said. Then, seeing her embarrassment, he added, "But it felt good in this heat. Hey!" He moved his hand to her shoulder. "Don't worry about it. I don't mind."

As his hand made contact with her bare skin, she reacted as though she had been burned. Jumping to her feet to hide her confusion, she said, "I'd better bring that dumb horse back."

She put her fingers to her lips and gave a shrill whistle. The horse pricked up his ears and headed toward them. Her rescuer towered above her, as they stood watching the horse padding slowly nearer.

Taking his reins, she turned to him. Feeling suddenly very self-conscious, she became very stiff and formal.

"Thank you. My name is Michelle Miller."

She pulled herself up on the horse's back, and he looked up at her, squinting against the sun. "Michelle, huh? You look more like a Mike to me."

"No one's ever told me that before," she said. "Mike's a boy's name."

"Well, you certainly don't remind me of a boy," he said, grinning. "Mike, I'm Rick McCord. It was fun going swimming with you. We'll have to do it again sometime."

To hide her embarrassment, she turned the horse and headed away at a fast clip. All the way back to the stable, she had repeated his name, through clenched teeth. "Rick McCord." So this was Connie's famous Rick McCord.

On Saturday her father flew in from New York. He demanded that the family look especially good for dinner at the Harbor House that evening.

"There's someone in town I want to talk with. We're meeting him tonight for dinner. Mary," he said to his wife, "be especially charming to him, dear. I think I'm going to get his account."

Michelle hurried to her room to dress for dinner, dreading the whole evening. She had been through these things so many times before. It meant spending the entire dinner hour watching the men out-brag each other, and watching the women trying to be charming even if they couldn't stand each other. Michelle knew that she would be expected to pay attention to the conversation in case one of the guests asked her a question when she least expected it. And it meant that she couldn't excuse herself and leave with her friends after dinner.

When they arrived at the Harbor House, they were shown to a table near the windows. Mr. Miller introduced his wife and daughters to the smiling couple already seated at the table. They were Mr. and Mrs. Martin McCord. Rick's parents.

While the men ordered drinks, Michelle buried herself behind her menu. Just as they were ordering dinner, Rick strolled over to the table and was introduced to the family. Grinning at Michelle, he pulled out a chair across from her sister Connie and picked up a menu. Michelle noticed the expression of delight on Connie's face and groaned inwardly.

The dinner went rather smoothly, considering that her father had already had three drinks, and Mr. McCord and his son glowered at each other over their meal. Mrs. McCord seemed pleasant enough, although she and Mrs. Miller hardly spoke. Connie bubbled with conversation, all of it aimed at Rick. He paid a great deal of attention to her and smiled at all the right moments. But once, Michelle noticed him glancing in her direction with the slightest quirk of his mouth, as though they shared a secret.

By the end of the evening Michelle was feeling miserable. Rick had asked Connie to dance three times, and their parents were gradually drinking too much and becoming louder. She wanted to slip away, but she knew her father would be furious. As Connie and Rick returned to the table, one of Rick's friends walked up and began to talk with him. He turned and introduced him to Connie. Immediately, the friend asked Connie to dance. She seemed about to refuse, but Rick turned at that moment, as though he might leave. Pausing for just a second, Connie accepted the offer to dance. As soon as they walked away, Rick turned and moved to Michelle's side.

Holding out his hand, he said softly, "Dance?"

She stood and put her hand in his. He led her across the dance floor toward the shadows. When he brought his arm around her, she felt a tiny shiver of pleasure. He had his arms around her. They moved slowly to the music, and Michelle could feel the warmth of his breath along her temple. His hand tightened along the small of her back, and she moved closer to him. She could feel his heartbeat through the thin fabric of her summer dress.

"Having fun?" he asked, and she shivered as his lips brushed her ear.

"Why certainly. Can't you tell?" she replied in her most sarcastic voice.

He threw back his head and laughed, a deep, rich sound. "Mike. You wear your feelings for the whole world to see. You can't hide them, can you?" he said.

She was suddenly defensive. "You mean I'm not laughing enough at Connie's silly chatter? Or batting my eyelashes enough at you, Mr. McCord? Is that what you mean?"

Rick looked down at her angry mouth set in a pout. "Oh, Mike. You do have a temper to match that fiery hair, don't you. I didn't mean anything of the kind. I just meant that you haven't learned yet how to act like the bored little rich kid, have you? Like your sister, Connie." He bent his head and rubbed his chin on her hair. "Maybe you'll be one of the lucky ones, who never learn."

When the music ended, Rick leaned down and whispered, "Let's get a breath of air."

He again took her hand, and led her across the wide back veranda and across the lawn toward the water's edge.

The full moon cast golden glimmers on the crest of the waves. An occasional sailboat was silhouetted on the horizon. Music drifted faintly down to the shore where they were standing.

Michelle had dated a few boys, although most of her escorts for school dances had been arranged by her parents. She had kissed most of the boys in her crowd, but she had never been kissed by a man before. As if reading her mind, Rick bent and touched his lips to hers tenderly. Then he lifted his head and gazed down at her. She had expected something different, and she looked up at him, puzzled. The breeze lifted a strand of her hair, and he reached out and smoothed it.

Then, running his finger down her cheek, he murmured, "Mike." He spoke the word like a caress.

She shivered slightly.

"You're still a tomboy, Mike," he whispered. "But part of you is a woman. Did you know that?"

Without warning, his hand slid around to the back of her neck, and he drew her to him. She gasped in surprise, and then his other arm wrapped around her, and she swayed against him weakly.

In her eighteen years, Michelle had never been kissed like that. As he continued to kiss her, she felt herself slowly responding to him. As though she would fall if she let go.

A tingling warmth spread through her limbs. It was a delicious, languorous feeling that she didn't want to end. Her senses seemed alive to Rick. She was aware of the faint smell of soap, and whiskey, and a new, unfamiliar male scent. She heard the trill of laughter and the muted sounds of music, carried from the dining room on the breeze. Somewhere, a boat horn sounded. A gull cried in the night. Michelle was suddenly aware of all of these things. And yet, none of them intruded on the moment. Every part of her seemed alive. Something had awakened in Michelle which she didn't understand, but which she nevertheless accepted. It was a stunning arousal.

But she couldn't let Rick know. To hide her feeling, she said breathlessly, "You shouldn't have kissed me like that! And you know it!"

Staring down at her, he replied, "Yes. I could tell you didn't like it."

She knew she hadn't fooled Rick with her feeble protest. He was aware of her response to his kiss. It would be foolish to pretend an outrage she didn't feel. She grew silent.

They stood, unmoving for long moments, until he again took her hand and began to walk slowly back toward the veranda.

In the next few weeks she saw Rick often, away from the crowd. They swam and rode horseback together, all the while arguing loudly about where to swim or ride. They rented a tandem bike and rode through the countryside, ending with a picnic in the woods. They had a violent argument—over what she could no longer recall—until a storm suddenly erupted. They rode home through pouring rain, thoroughly soaked, laughing hysterically. They walked to the ice cream shop in the evenings, or walked down the dark rutted roads, staring at the lights in the houses they passed.

They learned much about each other. Michelle confided to Rick how she adored her father, and how much she disliked her sister Connie, and how difficult it was to get along with her mother. She even admitted that she had hoped the summer would hurry and end, but she didn't add that all that had changed since she met Rick. She didn't trust herself to tell him too much yet.

Rick, in turn, confided to her that he and his father were locked in a bitter feud. His father was an executive with one of the auto companies. Rumor had it that he would be the next chairman of the board. Naturally, he planned to have Rick join him with the auto company. Rick had studied engineering in college, and that had made his parents happy. But he simply couldn't join the firm just to please his father. In fact, he was already experimenting with several things he thought he could develop on his own. But his father wouldn't hear of it. He really believed that if he kept fighting his son long enough, Rick would change his mind and join him. Rick was bitter, and said he had no intention of changing his mind.

That summer, Michelle's father succeeded in convincing Rick's father to invest with him. Michelle saw little of her father after that. He spent all his time rushing between his office in Detroit and another office in New York. But now that she had discovered Rick, Michelle didn't mind her father's absence nearly as much as before.

After the first time Rick kissed her, Michelle knew that she wanted him to hold her in his arms again. The few times after that that he did kiss her, it was the same for her. She felt the sparks of an emotion too strong for her to understand. But each time, just as she began to melt into his arms, Rick would suddenly become gruff, almost angry. Michelle felt certain it was her fault. She simply didn't know enough about all this. There was something she ought to do. But Rick would dismiss it, and angrily move away from her. A terrible tension was developing in their relationship; a tension Michelle didn't quite understand.

Her secure, familiar world, which Michelle had believed would never end, began to crumble in late August.

It was a Saturday night. Her mother was having dinner with friends before picking her father up at the station. Connie had left on a date. Michelle had been swinging on the back porch, dressed in old jean cut-offs and a soft white peasant shirt. It was a hot, sultry night, and she had slipped off her sandals and pulled down the elastic top around her shoulders. Rick suddenly appeared around the corner of the house and stood, staring at her. He had a strange look about him. Not quite angry. Not quite sad. A haunted look.

She smiled at him. "Hi Rick. Come on up here. Swing with me," she offered.

He walked toward her and stared down at her. As he sat down, she moved slightly nearer to him. The movement of the swing fanned her hair against his cheek. He slid his arm around her, then bent and touched his lips to her bare shoulder, giving her a prickly feeling down her spine. Abruptly, he stood up.

"Come on, Mike. Let's go for a walk." He held out his hand.

"It's so hot, Rick. Why not just sit here and swing?" she pleaded.

"Come on, Mike." It was a command.

Michelle bent and slipped on her sandals. Hand in hand, they walked down the road. They traveled more than a mile, from her house to the Winter Castle. Rick had grown quiet. Michelle was content just to be with him.

As they stopped outside the iron gate and stared at the lights of the mansion, Michelle whispered, "I love this old house. I guess it's my favorite in the whole town."

With his arm draped around her shoulder, he murmured, "Then I'll just have to buy it for you."

She chuckled, and he went on. "I know. As soon as we're ready to settle down, I'll come back and buy it for our honeymoon cottage."

"Honeymoon," she echoed in wonder.

Pressing his lips into her hair, he murmured, "Wouldn't it be fun to be mistress of this place?"

She turned and stared up at him dreamily. "If I married you it would."

"Look!" He pointed to the sky. "A shooting star! Make a wish."

She watched the path of light across the darkened sky, then squeezed her eyelids tight and wished.

On the walk back home, Rick said softly, "Mike. I'm going to have to leave Harbor Springs."

Swinging his hand, she replied, "You mean at the end of the summer."

"No," he said. "I mean soon. In a day or two."

She stopped in her tracks. "Rick! You can't!" she protested.

"Listen, Mike. Dad and I can never resolve our conflicts. There's no sense in my staying here and trying any longer. I only gave it another chance for my mother's sake. She hasn't been well for years now, and this rift in the family has been tearing her up. But it isn't working out. My being here is just making things worse between Mom and Dad. Mike," he said turning her to face him. "I made a few phone calls this evening, before I came to see you. I've got some designs in my mind that I'm positive will work. But in order to experiment, I need my lab. So I've set things up with my engineering firm back in Texas."

He took her hand, and they continued walking back to her darkened house. At the back door, she asked him to come in. They were both tense and edgy.

"No. Your folks will be home soon. I'm not in the mood to talk to them. Or to anybody. Except you, Mike. I needed to talk to you."

Michelle turned, fighting the tears welling up in her eyes, and walked slowly toward the rose arbor. It was a small arch, completely covered with fragrant roses in bloom. As Rick moved up closer to her, Michelle suddenly threw her arms around Rick's neck and began to cry.

"Please, Rick, don't leave! I love you! I really do!" she sobbed.

He gently wiped her tears with his thumbs, whispering, "Shhh. Mike. You don't even know what love is yet."

"Don't I?" she cried. "I know that I'll never feel about any man the way I feel about you. I don't want you to leave me, Rick." She began to cry harder.

He kissed away the tears and, as his mouth closed over hers, she could taste the salt of her tears on his lips. As her tears stopped, he continued kissing her, parting her lips and kissing her more urgently. A tiny flame of passion began in the pit of her stomach, making her feel weak. As he pulled his head away from her, Michelle leaned closer and buried her lips in his neck. She felt his quick intake of breath and, suddenly aware of what effect she had on him, she stood on tiptoe and brought her lips around to the hollow between his neck and his muscular shoulder. Without warning, she was locked in a grip of steel. They both dropped to their knees, then, gently, Michelle and Rick were lying on the grass in the fragrant rose arbor. His hand moved to the elastic neckline of her peasant blouse, and he probed the sensitive skin of her throat. When he brought his lips down to touch the rounded curve of her breast, she was carried on a tide of passion which she could not control. As she brought her body tightly against his, she let out a little moan.

Angrily, Rick rolled away from her. She knelt up and put her hand on his shoulder.

"Rick?" she whispered.

"Mike, don't touch me," he growled.

"What have I done, Rick?" she asked.

"Mike!" he hissed, and as he looked at her he added, "Pull up your blouse."

As she fumbled with the elastic of her blouse, he sat up and wearily ran a hand through his mussed hair.

Then, slowly, in a tightly controlled voice, he said, "Look, Mike. You have a lot of things you have to do. Four years of college. Four years! And I have to prove to myself that I can make it without my father's help." He took her hands and gazed into her eyes. "Mike, I . . . I really care about you. A lot. But four years from now, when you've finished college, you might have an altogether different idea about who you love."

"Rick!" she protested. "I won't change my mind about you. I'm going to marry you, and we're going to live in the Winter Castle. You promised!"

"Shhh." He put his fingers tenderly over her lips. "A lot can happen in a few years," he said. "Who knows. The next time I see you, you might be married and have six kids."

"I'm not going to marry anyone else," she vowed.

"You'd better not, or I'll . . ." He leaned closer and kissed her lightly on her forehead. "Anyway, Mike, we came very close to spoiling something special tonight. We do have something special, you know." He kissed the tip of her nose. "But I'm twenty-eight, Mike, and you're the most sheltered eighteen-year-old I've ever met." His voice became gruff. "I'd hate myself if I ever spoiled—what you are." Standing abruptly, he added, "Now I've got to go."

He helped her up, and they clung to each other.

"Rick. Will you come and see me tomorrow?" she asked.

"Wild horses couldn't keep me away," he called lightly.

Michelle watched as Rick walked away, then she let herself in the back door.

Connie's shrill voice pierced the darkness. "You filthy little tramp! I saw you and Rick in the grass."

Michelle whirled in the darkness. "Connie! What are you doing home with the lights off?"

"Watching you, little innocent sister! Daddy's little darling Missy! And with Rick McCord!"

"What would you know about Rick McCord!" cried Michelle.

"A whole lot more than you, baby sister." Connie snapped on the light and faced Michelle, her hands on her hips, her eyes glittering angrily. "Sweet little Missy. You're just one in a long string of girls. Old love 'em and leave 'em Rick can have any girl he wants," she taunted.

As the front door opened, her parents strode in and her father said, "What in the world are you two shouting about? Your mother and I could hear you clear out in the driveway."

Connie's eyes narrowed, and she stared triumphantly at Michelle. Then, pretending sadness, she answered, "Daddy and Mamma. I know this is going to hurt you both, but for Michelle's own protection, I just have to tell you what I saw with my own eyes tonight."

Michelle had stood paralyzed as Connie pro-

ceeded to describe what she had seen at the rose
arbor. Her mother's hand shot up to her mouth in
shocked surprise. Her father's eyes had narrowed,
and his mouth was a thin line of unchecked anger.

"But Dad. It's not what you think!" Michelle
protested.

"Go to your room, Missy," he ordered.

"No! Dad! I have to explain. You have to listen!"
she rasped. "We didn't do anything wrong. Rick
wouldn't do anything, ever, to hurt me!"

"Go! Now!" His fist pounded the table, sending a
vase flying. "Or, I swear, Michelle, I'll kill you!"

She fled to her room, sobbing. She had never seen
her father in a rage before. Downstairs, she could
hear her parents and Connie shouting, their voices
raised in a violent argument. Much later, the front
door slammed. The house grew quiet. In the small
hours of the morning, exhausted from crying,
Michelle slept fitfully.

In the morning, she was greeted by silent accusing
stares from her mother and Connie. Her father did
not come downstairs until almost noon. He looked
haggard and refused to speak to her. Michelle sat on
the back porch swing, waiting all that day for Rick to
come. He never appeared.

That evening, she walked past his house. She
could see Rick and his father, silhouetted against the
shade in the library. She stood outside the house as
long as she dared; but Rick never came out.

Sorrow wrapped itself around Michelle's heart
like a vise. *He isn't going to come back to see me* she
thought. *I've spoiled it all. Like a fool, I told him I*

loved him. I've ruined everything. How he must be laughing at me.

Connie's sarcastic voice taunted her. "Dad went to see Rick and his family. He ordered Rick to stay away from his virginal little darling, or he'd cause plenty of trouble. And you know Dad's temper. You had a taste of it the other night."

On Monday morning Michelle was awakened very early by loud voices. Climbing out of bed, she threw on a summer robe and padded down the stairs to the hallway. As she poked her head around the corner, she heard her father's voice, protesting angrily. She stared in amazement. There were photographers, reporters, uniformed police, all milling about the front porch and foyer. Her mother was seated on a bench, sobbing. Her father grabbed his suit jacket and left, surrounded by the swarms of people.

On the floor, lying face up, was the morning newspaper. In bold headlines she saw her father's name, and an old official photo of him. Dropping to her knees, she read the paper quickly. Looking up at her mother, her face buried in her hands, Michelle felt the need to protect her. She ran to her side and put her arms around her. The headlines had stated in bold letters that her father had been accused of embezzlement and stock manipulation. His accuser was Martin McCord.

In the days to come, the scandal rocked not only the town of Harbor Springs, but the nation as well.

Michelle, Connie and their mother packed and fled from Harbor Springs as soon as they could. They left Rose and Lon and a few servants to close up The

Oaks. Mr. Miller promised to follow them after his appearance at his arraignment with his lawyers.

Michelle was racked with doubts. Had her father really commited these terrible crimes he'd been accused of? Or was Martin McCord, stung by her father's horrible threats to Rick, just getting even in his own cruel way?

A phone call from Rose several days later caused Mrs. Miller to collapse. Taking the phone from her mother's grip, Connie asked, "What is it, Rose?"

Hearing the news, she handed the phone to Michelle and began to sob. Michelle listened as Rose explained that she and Lon had discovered Mr. Miller's body in his bedroom. In his anguish, unable to bear the enormity of his crime, he had returned alone to The Oaks and put a gun to his head.

So her father actually was guilty. It had not merely been some fabrication on Martin McCord's part.

The months which followed were buried under layers of pain for Michelle.

Her mother had been unable to accept the responsibility for even the simplest decision. Connie had taken to her room, sulking. And so it fell to Michelle to assume responsibility for all their lives.

She ordered Rose to close the house in Harbor Springs and return her father's body for burial. Afterward, the insurance company refused to pay any benefits because of her father's death by his own hand. This necessitated selling off as much as possible to pay off their enormous debts.

A real estate agent in Harbor Springs found a buyer for The Oaks. Rose and Lon spent weeks packing up the furniture and valuables which were sold at auction.

Michelle notified all the servants that she could no longer afford them. She gave them all excellent references, and they were soon hired by friends and neighbors of the Millers, who knew of their record of fine service.

Mrs. Miller became an invalid, refusing to even attempt to leave her bed.

In frustration, Connie demanded to be allowed to complete her final year of college, reasoning that she could then return home and work while Michelle began her college education the following year. Michelle agreed to stay home for the year and work and care for her mother.

Within the year, however, her mother died, and Connie fled after graduation to California, to begin a new life.

After her mother's death, Michelle sold the large house in Detroit and moved to a small apartment. She took a job with the Forest Corporation, working during the day and attending college at night.

Her life had changed so dramatically, it was a wonder Michelle even survived.

Now, suddenly throwing off the covers, Michelle strode from the bed and looked over the clothes she had brought with her for the weekend. As she dressed, she thought again about the man she would have to face downstairs. Every time she thought about the silly, artless girl she had been with him, she felt humiliated. How he must have laughed when he left Harbor Springs. How could a worldly, twenty-eight-year-old man like Rick McCord have found her eighteen-year-old ignorance anything but amusing! And when he had realized what her father had done to his father and the other investors, he must have been furious to have been associated with her in any way. Fool that she was, she had waited, still believing that he would contact her. And for months, even years after, she had nurtured a small flicker of hope that Rick would somehow contact her and declare his undying love despite all that had happened between their families.

But now Michelle had put aside all her childish hopes of the romantic hero who would come to her rescue. In place of those hopes, she had faced reality. She was, she thought, like a cat who, no matter how many times it gets tossed from a secure spot, lands on its feet. She had painfully learned the art of survival.

As she glanced at her reflection in the mirror, she smiled grimly. Tonight, there must be no trace of the silly schoolgirl she had once been. Mr. Rick McCord would see a woman, calm and secure, who was accustomed to dealing with men like him in business. And if she had to look into those cold, steel eyes of his, she wouldn't flinch. If she could convince him that he meant nothing more to her than any other man in the room, perhaps she could even consider working with him. After all, it was only for a short time. She shivered. But even if she could convince him that he meant nothing to her, could she convince herself?

Chapter Three

At nine o'clock Michelle, dressed in a pale green silk dress with a jade green mohair jacket, descended the wide stairs and entered a room where she heard voices. Several men looked up in surprise at the breathtakingly beautiful woman in green, whose soft auburn hair settled about her face and shoulders like a silken red cloud.

She glanced over the faces, smiling, until she located Jim Bannon's friendly face. Walking toward her, he gave her an admiring smile.

Jim's white hair, a shocking contrast to his tanned, ruddy complexion, was carefully groomed. He was dressed in his business attire, a dark vested suit with a carefully knotted tie. She knew by the way he gently touched her arm that he wanted to act as a buffer between her and the strangers in the room who had come to look her over. She stared up at him, smiling warmly.

"Right on time," he said, "and looking especially lovely."

"Thank you sir," she said, dimpling.

She was aware that Rick was coming toward them, but she refused to look directly at him. Instead, she turned her head, as though to speak to Jim. When she felt Rick directly at her side, she turned her head slowly, putting off the moment when she would have to look into those eyes. He was wearing a navy suede blazer over gray flannel slacks. His light blue shirt was casually open at the throat, exposing a few dark hairs curling upward from his chest. She forced herself to meet his cold eyes.

"Good evening, Rick," she said softly.

"Mike. I believe you drink wine," he said, handing her a long stemmed glass.

"Thank you. Is everyone here?" she asked, glad to look away from him to the faces around the room.

"Everyone except my lawyer. He'll be along. In the meantime, come and meet some of my associates."

Without touching her, he walked by her side, stopping to introduce her to the men around the room. From the deference they showed Rick, there was no doubt in Michelle's mind who was in command here.

Michelle realized suddenly that she was the only woman there. "Your wives aren't with you on this trip?" she asked the two men who had been just introduced to her.

Rick interrupted. "Yes, they're along. But since tonight is strictly business, I knew the wives would rather not be bothered. Tomorrow night, though, we'll have dinner with all of them," he added.

Of course, she realized with a start. *Rick could be married. And his wife is probably entertaining the wives at a dinner in town.* The thought disturbed her and she had to force herself to concentrate on the names of the men she was meeting.

Turning toward the doorway, Rick said, "Ah. Burt. Michelle, my lawyer, Burt Matheson."

She turned in the direction of a tall, thin man with sharp hawklike eyes and a warm smile.

"Michelle!" the elderly man exclaimed in surprise, smiling broadly at her.

"Burt. How have you been?" she asked as she rushed to hug him.

Seeing the surprised look Rick gave this warm reception, Burt Matheson explained, "I was the lawyer for Michelle's family until . . . for many years," he amended awkwardly.

"I see," said Rick, staring at them both.

"My dear," Burt said, taking her hand, "it's wonderful to see you looking so beautiful. Anna and I have missed you," he added gently.

After handing Burt a drink, the frowning young Asian bartender left the room and returned a few moments later. Whispering to Rick, he again left the room.

"Dinner is ready, gentlemen," Rick said. Turning to Michelle, he added, "Mike," his mouth set in a thin line. When he offered her his arm, Michelle had no choice but to accept. Although she kept her touch as light as possible, she could feel the hard muscles of his arm through the soft suede fabric of his jacket.

He held her chair, then sat to her left, at the head of the table. The others took seats around the long banquet table. While they ate, Rick kept his face averted from Michelle. Whenever he spoke, he directed his conversation to everyone at the table, deliberately refusing to look directly at her. Michelle was painfully aware that Rick was ignoring her. She spoke as little as possible, hoping to avoid drawing attention to herself.

Midway through the excellent dinner, Michelle turned to him. "If I didn't know better, I'd swear that Henri LaRue cooked this dinner," she said quietly.

"What do you mean 'if you didn't know better'?" he asked, raising one eyebrow.

"I remember that Henri never caters private affairs," she answered.

"This is his off-season. Henri was more than happy to oblige," said Rick, staring coolly at her.

"If he's still here later, I'd love to see him, just for a moment, to say hello and compliment him on this lovely dinner," she said, feeling suddenly shy.

"I'm sure he'll be pleased," said Rick. "I'll see to it." Then he again turned and directed his conversation to the guests at the table.

After dessert and coffee, Michelle found herself being questioned rather thoroughly by Rick's associates. He himself had little to ask, but he leaned back and observed. Michelle was certain that his brain was recording everything that was said. When the group finally arose and made their way to the library, where they intended to discuss the merger further, Rick caught Michelle's arm and said quietly, "Come with me, and I'll take you to the kitchen."

Walking behind him, she entered the kitchen where Henri and two young men were noisily cleaning up.

As he turned and caught sight of Michelle, Henri stared in surprise for several seconds before coming toward her. With his arms outstretched, he exclaimed, "It is Michelle Miller, is it not! My dear! How have you been?"

"Very well, Henri," she said. "I recognized the excellent cooking as yours, and wanted to come here to compliment you. And to say hello," she added.

Henri beamed. Then, taking her hand and seeing the wedding band, he exclaimed, "Well, Rick, I see our little tomboy has grown up. And you are here tonight, Michelle, as the wife of one of Rick's friends, eh?"

"No," she assured him quickly. "I'm here on business."

"And we'd better not keep them waiting too much longer," said Rick abruptly.

"Good night, Henri," she called. "The dinner was lovely."

"Good night, my dear," he replied.

As Michelle walked along the hallway toward the library, she was conscious of Rick's imposing figure directly behind her. As they came to the library, he reached around her to open the door. She brushed past his arm and held herself stiffly.

Once in the library, the atmosphere was much more relaxed. The men were smoking and enjoying brandy. There was a fire laid against the chilly autumn night. Michelle answered several questions directed to her and opened the pages of memos which she had brought with her. She spread these out on Rick's massive oak desk and discreetly moved away so that the men could feel free to examine them. Then she settled into a comfortable chair drawn up near the fire, and watched and listened as the men discussed the details of the proposed merger.

As the talk drifted around her, Michelle allowed her thoughts to turn to Rick McCord. She had managed to keep up with his successes quite easily. He was often written about in newspapers and news magazines.

A year or two after her mother's death, Michelle had read about Rick's work in Houston. He had designed a device which revolutionized the space industry. That single design had brought him instant fame. He then modified it to be used on commercial aircraft. She had read that the device he invented had stabilized the craft in such a way that no amount of outside pressure could cause rolling or pitching— a common problem on spacecraft and airplanes alike. He had since bought out several large engineering and design firms.

Rumor had been rampant in Detroit that Rick

McCord would now turn his genius toward the auto industry. Since his father, who had achieved his dream of becoming chairman of the board of one auto company, was now dead, there would be no hint of conflict of interest. And the industry was desperate to come up with much needed energy conservation devices. The logical solution was to encourage someone with Rick's imagination to solve the problem.

Michelle had often seen Rick's picture in the papers. Occasionally, at some charity event or glittering social function, he would be photographed with a beautiful woman. As far as she knew, there had not been a marriage written about. But, of course, she realized that Rick would be capable of keeping a romance away from the public eye. Hadn't he kept this company name a secret? And certainly the press seemed unaware that Erick McCord was living in Harbor Springs. Apparently, Rick valued his privacy.

Annoyed at the way her thoughts had drifted, Michelle tossed her head angrily, as though to dispel any further thought of Rick McCord. The movement caused her fiery hair to dance about her face and settle like a burnished cloud about her shoulders. The strands of hair reflected the dancing flames of the fire which blazed beside her. As she turned her head, she saw Rick across the room, staring intently at her as the man at his elbow continued talking.

Several times during the evening, she met Jim Bannon's eyes and smiled reassuringly. He returned the smile. As the night wore on, Michelle felt herself relaxing. Though the men had questioned her thoroughly, they seemed satisfied with her answers.

While they discussed a minor point of the merger, she arose and walked to a small cabinet to look more closely at some of the objects on display. As she stood there, she sensed that Rick was behind her. Half-turning, she accepted a glass from his outstretched hand.

"I thought you might want this," he said. He was staring intently at her.

"Thank you," she murmured.

As she sipped the wine, he continued to stare at her, his eyes boring through her skin. Then he stiffened slightly and said, "I noticed you were interested in my collection."

Slowly, he began describing the various shells and small sculptures displayed in the cabinet. He was standing so near, she could feel his breath fan her temple. Once, as she bent to see an odd-shaped piece of coral, she felt her shoulder brush his arm. She had to force herself to listen to his description of the various items. She asked him about one of the shells, and as she turned to glance at him, his eyes were still fastened on her. She realized that Rick must have traveled all over the world. Each of the shells and sculptures was from an entirely unrelated area.

Within the hour, the men were saying their goodbyes. Alone in the library for a few minutes, while Rick walked to the front door with his guests, Jim turned to Michelle and winked.

"I think it went well. Don't you agree?" he asked.

She smiled, but before she could reply, Rick had returned to the library.

"Would either of you care for a nightcap?" he asked.

"No, thank you, Rick," said Jim Bannon. "I'm afraid the long drive really did me in. If you don't mind, I'm going up to bed."

Panic at the thought of being trapped into staying alone with Rick made Michelle suddenly add, "I'll walk up with you, Jim."

Turning to Rick, she said, 'Good night, Rick."

Then she moved quickly along at Jim's side. As they climbed the stairs, she could feel Rick's eyes following her.

Alone in her room, Michelle lay for hours trying to sleep. But she couldn't forget the fact that she was really here, in the Winter Castle, and that somewhere in this same house, Erick McCord was sleeping. Rick, master of this old house.

In the morning, Michelle sat up in bed and realized that the temperature had dropped during the night. The room was cold. She showered and dressed quickly in a soft beige wool suit and a white cashmere sweater under the jacket. She brushed her hair until it gleamed, and applied very little makeup. Slipping quietly down the stairs, she headed for the kitchen. As she opened the door, she nearly collided with the man who had been the bartender the night before.

"Oh. Good morning," she said. "I didn't know if anyone was up yet."

"Good morning, Miss. You tell me what you like. I fix," he said frowning.

"Just coffee, thanks. If you'll show me where it is, I'll get it myself," she offered.

"No. You go dining room. I bring coffee," he ordered.

Michelle walked to the dining room, smiling to herself at the Asian's determination to rule his kitchen. She stopped abruptly when she realized she wasn't alone. Rick and Jim Bannon were having breakfast.

"Good morning. You look cheerful," said Jim.

"I was laughing at Rick's houseman. He ordered me out of his kitchen."

"Trang is a dictator in that kitchen," said Rick. "He was having fits last night because Henri and his crew took over. Today he'll be a bear to live with. But by tomorrow, he will be back to normal," Rick said calmly.

Rick held her chair for her. As she sat, he asked, "How did you sleep?"

"Very well. The room is lovely, Rick. It has a fabulous view of the lake," she said.

"Yes. I know. I thought you'd like it," he added with an edge to his voice.

"Rick. Did your corporation buy this house as an investment?" Jim asked him.

"No. I bought it," Rick answered. He seemed about to say more, then suddenly he clamped his mouth shut.

Michelle noticed that in the bright morning light his face appeared more angular, even harsher than the previous night. There were tight lines around his eyes and mouth.

Unable to sit quietly under his scrutiny, Michelle stood abruptly and walked to the windows. She stared out at the spacious grounds, overgrown with weeds, and kept her back to the men at the table until Trang entered the room, carrying a tray loaded with toast, jelly and a steaming pot of coffee. He hovered about the table, pouring coffee, offering toast and jelly, asking what more they might need. When he finally left the room, Jim Bannon smiled.

"He's certainly conscientious, isn't he?" he commented, glancing from Rick to Michelle.

"Trang is indispensable," agreed Rick.

Glancing up, Jim asked, "Have you scheduled a meeting today with everyone?"

Rick stirred his coffee and remarked, "I thought we'd meet today with just Burt, my lawyer, and one or two of the others. I've asked the rest of my associates to go over the papers you brought with you. That way, they can note any questions they may have and jot down any areas that they think need clarification. Tomorrow, we'll have a final meeting with everyone. Most of the men have to get back by tomorrow night. I think you will have answered their questions and ironed out any difficult issues by then. What's left, can then be handled in the weeks to come."

Michelle had listened to this with only half her mind. She was determined to find some time alone with Jim. She had to explain how she happened to know Rick and to explain why Jim might not want her to handle this merger for him. This would be disappointing for Jim. He had worked so long and hard for this. And he was so confident of her abilities. She knew this was going to be a terrible letdown.

Now she realized grimly that Jim was talking to Rick about her, praising her.

"I could see that your associates were impressed with Michelle's answers last night," Jim was saying.

Michelle glanced up guiltily and caught Jim's eye. But he was not to be deterred. Smiling at her, he plunged on.

"Michelle was old Joe Forest's right-hand aide. In his last days, Michelle kept things going smoothly almost single-handedly. And when I was brought in, she eased me into the job as though I'd always been handling it."

She lowered her eyes and gritted her teeth as she self-consciously stirred her coffee. Finally, her cheeks flushed, she forced herself to meet Rick's gaze. He was staring at her with an arrogant expression.

"You sound like a proud Papa, Jim," he commented.

"I guess I do," admitted Jim. "But I wanted you to know how hard she's worked on this merger for us, and how proud we are of her work."

Michelle stood abruptly. "If you're through with the flattery, Jim," she said, trying to keep her voice light, "I think we need to get together for a little while—to discuss a few things."

"Oh, I'm sorry, Mike," interrupted Rick. "I told

Jim earlier that he was expected at the Harbor House for an early meeting before we get together here this afternoon." He arose, and Jim followed suit. "By the way, Mike," Rick added, "I've asked the men to bring their wives to dinner tonight. They're all dying to see you."

To Jim, he added, "I'll have Mac drive you to the Harbor House. He's taking Trang into town for some things. Burt Matheson will bring you back when he comes. Ready?" he asked, and strode from the room.

Jim patted Michelle's arm and turned to go.

"Jim!" she called, suddenly feeling panic at the thought of being left alone with Rick.

"Yes?" He turned and smiled, waiting for her to continue.

She bit her lower lip and frowned, then, smiling with a forced brightness, she shook her head. "Nothing," she said. "Have a good morning."

Michelle gulped her coffee as she heard the front door slam. Intending to hurry upstairs to her room, she turned toward the doorway, and stopped. Rick was leaning against the door, his arms folded across his chest, his dark eyes glinting. Looking at him, Michelle felt her heart begin to hammer. It was as though the clock had been turned back. He looked as he had looked years ago, when he was about to goad her into an argument.

Well, Mike, I . . ."

"Don't call me that!" she snapped.

He raised one eyebrow as he walked closer to her. Sarcastically, he said with great emphasis, "Mrs.

Scott, I thought you might want to look over the counter-proposals I had drawn up for you. If you'll follow me to the library." He bowed dramatically from the waist and walked quickly from the room.

She hurried after him, gritting her teeth. The only sounds in the house were the rapid tattoo of her high heels along the hallway.

A cozy fire had been started in the library. Rick moved to his desk and opened a file folder. He handed the papers across his desk to Michelle, then sat down and watched her closely as she read them. Though she tried to concentrate on the words, she was too aware of his eyes on her. Finally, in exasperation, she stood.

"I hope you don't mind, Rick. I'd like to take these somewhere alone, where I can concentrate."

"No, no, Mrs. Scott," he said evenly. "Go ahead and concentrate here. I'll find something else to do." And with that, he crossed the room and tossed another log on the fire. He picked up a poker and began stirring up the flames.

Michelle sat back down and began to read. In a few minutes, she had completely forgotten Rick. Half an hour later, she set down the last page and turned. Rick was leaning against the fireplace, one arm resting on the stone mantle. Her heart lurched at the strange, yet familiar look on his face. Not quite angry. Not quite sad. A haunted look. When he realized she was watching him, he straightened and instantly the look was gone. He returned to his desk and assumed an air of professional interest.

"Well?" he asked. "Do you approve?"

"With most of it," she answered. "But there are several things here," she said, pointing.

Rick walked around the desk and stood behind her chair, reading where she pointed. "Yes," he said, nodding. "I see what you mean. I think some changes are in order."

He walked back to his desk and pulled a second chair next to hers. Side by side they worked, exchanging ideas and rewording phrases, until they were satisfied with the way it read. Rick glanced at his watch. Nearly two hours had passed since they began. He set down his papers and looked at Michelle.

"We work well together. How about stopping for some lunch, Mike?"

"I told you not to call me that, Rick," she hissed.

"Why not? You call me Rick," he said, a hint of a smile vanishing instantly from his lips.

"That's different. Mike sounds so . . . familiar," she said.

"Oh, I see. You mean 'what will all the others think?' Is that it?" he said dryly.

"Something like that. I haven't even had a chance to explain to Jim Bannon—about us. I'm sure he's a little puzzled," she said softly.

Rick scraped back his chair and stood abruptly, towering above her. "I don't give a damn what Jim Bannon or the others think."

He walked to the door and turned. "If you're hungry, there's plenty of food in the kitchen. The meeting this afternoon is here in the library at two o'clock. If you'll excuse me, I have work to do, Mrs. Scott." He turned and walked down the hall.

Michelle stormed to the kitchen. Trang was not there. She assumed he was still in town shopping for the dinner tonight. A glance in the refrigerator assured her there was plenty to eat. She made herself a salad and put the kettle on for tea. Waiting for the water to boil, she thought about Rick. She was surprised that they had worked so well together. Although in the beginning she had felt awkward, she had soon forgotten about the nearness of him. And while they had discussed the wording of the proposals, she had discovered that he was fair and agreeable. If she could just get over her personal feelings, she knew she could work with him on this project. Oh, it would make Jim so unhappy if she backed out now! He was counting on her. If she had only kept her mouth shut in the library when Rick called her Mike. Frowning, she walked to the stove and poured the water into a teapot. But she had to hold him at a distance. Every time she heard Rick use that knickname, her stomach turned into knots. He had no idea what he was doing to her nerves.

As Michelle turned from the stove, she was so startled she nearly spilled the tea. Rick was standing in the doorway, staring at her.

He thrust his hands deep into the pockets of his corduroy pants and sauntered across the kitchen.

"I see you made tea," he said. "I'd prefer coffee, but I'll drink anything, as long as it's hot."

He reached into a cupboard for a cup, and

Michelle watched the flannel shirt stretch taut across the muscles of his back and shoulders. He sat across the table from her and poured himself a cup of tea. Glancing at her salad, he asked, "What's in that? It looks good."

As she told him, he brought out all the ingredients from the refrigerator and began to expertly make himself a similar salad. When it was ready, he again sat down and tasted it.

"It's good," he said. "How about some cheese?" Without waiting for her reply, he again stood and brought out cheese and crackers. They ate and talked, and soon were smiling across the table. It was as though they had declared a temporary truce.

"I'm glad Trang wasn't here to frown at us," said Michelle. "I suppose he's shopping for tonight's dinner."

"Oh, dinner isn't here tonight," Rick said. "I thought you might like to see what they've done to the Harbor House in the past few years. We're having cocktails here, and a few appetizers. It's really just an excuse for the wives to get a chance to look over the house. They've been dropping hints that they're curious about this old place. Then, we'll drive back to the Harbor House for dinner. Henri has been putting up most of the men and their wives, and he's eager to do something special. Of course," he said with a smile, "Trang's pouting. But he'll do something spectacular for the cocktail hour, I'm sure."

"Where did you find Trang?" she asked.

"Trang is from Vietnam. He was one of the

homeless 'boat people.' I was in the Philippines when their boat was allowed to land. After he was processed, he needed a sponsor to get to the States."

"And you needed a cook?" she asked.

"Not really," he said, grinning. "What I needed was someone around to fight with." He pushed back his chair and stretched out his long legs. He regarded her with lazy insolence and added, "Now if you were to stick around for a while, Trang would find out he's no match for your sharp tongue."

Michelle stood abruptly, and clattered the dirty dishes noisily in the sink. As she poured in detergent and turned on the taps, Rick picked up a towel and stood next to her.

Glancing at him, she bit back a sharp retort and said instead, "I don't think Trang would like to find his kitchen full of dirty dishes."

"Good thinking. You wash, I'll dry." He picked up the first dripping cup and expertly dried it and hung it in the cupboard.

"There was a time when you wouldn't have even thought of washing dishes, Mike. The servants would have done it all for you," he said matter-of-factly.

"I've had to learn how to do a lot of things for myself, Rick," she said. She tried to keep her voice even as she asked the one question she had wanted to ask since the thought first came to her the night before. "Will your wife be here tonight, Rick?"

His hand paused in midair for an instant, then his voice took on a harsh edge. "There's no wife, Mike."

They were just finishing up when they heard the back door open, and Trang entered, carrying a heavy grocery bag.

Stopping in his tracks, he croaked, "You allow Miss work in my kitchen!"

His jet black eyes were like two dark storm clouds. He was no taller than Michelle, and he reminded her of a little bantam rooster.

Drying her hands on a towel, she said as cheerfully as she could, "We didn't disturb a thing, Trang."

Rick's look softened and he took her by the elbow. As they reached the door, he turned and said, "Remember, Trang. Cocktails at seven o'clock."

Then they turned and flew down the hallway, chuckling for a moment like two conspirators.

Chapter Four

The afternoon meeting dragged on interminably. Burt Matheson had several points he wanted to discuss in great detail. Jim and Michelle went over them carefully with him, but he seemed unhappy with the phrasing of several points, and again and again he and his associates went back over the issue until they were satisfied.

Michelle noticed that Rick seemed willing to sit back and let Burt and the others do most of the talking. But she had the distinct impression that the questions being asked were the ones Rick wanted answered, and that he was the only one they had to worry about keeping entirely satisfied.

After their temporary respite at lunch, Michelle and Rick once again slipped into their roles of highly skilled adversaries.

Several times, when she explained her company position, or defined a particular employment policy, she noticed Rick's lips quirk slightly, as though suppressing a smile.

Was he laughing at her, she wondered angrily. Then, as if to dismiss all thoughts of Rick from her mind, she shook her head in that familiar, defiant gesture, which she often used unconsciously. She was not aware that the unaffected gesture caused her hair to fan out in a silken flaming cloud about her face and shoulders. Rick's eyes followed the motion of her hair. Then his eyes narrowed as he concentrated on the discussion going on around him.

Michelle was keeping a close watch on the time. Jim Bannon and Burt Matheson and the others had arrived just in time for the meeting, having eaten lunch at the Harbor House. There had been no time for her to confer with Jim about how the morning meeting had gone. And she desperately wanted to find time to talk to Jim about her previous relationship with Rick. She was determined that Jim be completely informed about it, in case he felt that she should be removed from this position of importance.

Michelle was relieved when, promptly at five o'clock, Rick arose and said, "Gentlemen." Then, nodding at Michelle, he added, "Mrs. Scott. We'll adjourn for today. Cocktails at seven. I'll see all of you back here then."

His formal use of her name hadn't gone unnoticed by her. She smiled in silent gratitude.

The men packed up their briefcases and headed toward the door. As Jim arose, Michelle caught his arm and said, "Wait for a few minutes, Jim. I need to talk to you."

Rick escorted the others to the front door, and Michelle turned to Jim. "I wanted to ask you how the meeting went this morning. And I also need to talk to you about something else. Would you like to talk here, or would you prefer to talk upstairs, in your room?"

As he was about to reply, Rick returned.

Turning to Rick, Jim said, "Is there some place Michelle and I could hold an informal meeting for a little while, Rick?"

Rick glanced at Michelle, then, seeing the tight set of her mouth, he shrugged. "How about right here?" he suggested. "I have things to do anyway. I'll see you two downstairs around seven." Then, without waiting for their reply, he closed the library doors and left them alone.

Jim sat down near the fireplace and indicated the chair across from him. Michelle slumped down and stared at her hands.

"Come on, Michelle," he said. "What's the problem?"

"Well, Jim, I've been hoping to talk to you. To explain about Rick McCord. I mean, surely you were aware that we knew each other."

"Yes. I'd noticed," he replied. Then he shrugged. "What about it? So you both spent your summers here. Is there some problem, Michelle?"

"Well, yes," she said, suddenly feeling rather foolish. Just what was she going to say to Jim? That she once loved Rick McCord? That she felt awkward and uncomfortable around him? That he was aware of her family scandal?

Licking her dry lips, she began again. "Jim, Rick and I were once . . ."

She spread her hands in a hopeless gesture. She simply couldn't say it.

Trying to help her, Jim interrupted, "You two were once involved in a summer romance?"

"Well, yes," she said weakly.

"How long ago was this?" he asked.

"Six years ago," she answered.

"Let's see. You would have been . . . eighteen. Well? Is that it? I mean, just a summer thing? You weren't engaged, or—anything serious, were you?"

Michelle fidgeted. This was humiliating. "No. No engagement—or anything. But, one other thing. It was Rick's father who accused my father in the stock scandal."

"I see." He waited patiently for her to go on, his mouth clamped shut on anything more he might have wanted to say, and stared calmly at her. Finally, he asked, "Has Rick brought it up? Has he suggested that he would rather not work with you on this deal?"

Michelle twisted her hands in her lap and stared down at the floor for several long seconds. "No, Jim. Nothing like that. He's really been decent about all of this. He hasn't mentioned a thing about my father. I don't think he can bring himself to do that. It's just—I thought you deserved to know that we . . . go back a long way together. I thought you might want to reconsider having me work on this project."

Jim reached across and took her cold hands. "Michelle. I hate to ask this, but you seem so upset. Was there more than you've told me? I mean, did you have an affair with Rick McCord?"

"Oh, no, Jim. I never meant . . ."

"All right then. I'm sorry, but I didn't see any way to be delicate about that. It's just—I had to be sure what we're talking about. Look, Michelle, I don't see how an old summer romance should get in the way of your job. It happens to a lot of people. We run into someone we once dated. But McCord certainly doesn't strike me as the kind of guy who would judge you guilty for your father's crime. Unless there's more to it than you've told me, I don't see where any of this should be a problem for either you or Rick. Do you?"

He was staring intently at her, and Michelle faced him.

Finally she shook her head. "Of course not, Jim. It was a long time ago. But I thought you should know." She smiled weakly. "Thanks, Jim." Then, squaring her shoulders, she asked, "How did the meeting go this morning?"

"It went well," he assured her. "I think most of the men approve of the preliminary work you've done on this merger. I don't foresee many problems." He stood. "Let's go upstairs. I need to unwind before dinner."

Michelle climbed the stairs beside Jim, feeling

relieved that they had finally found time to talk. Jim was right, of course, she thought. What could a summer romance of six years ago possibly mean to either of the parties involved?

At the top of the stairs, Jim patted her shoulder before turning to his room. She moved on to her room, stopping suddenly when a door to her left opened, and Rick stood framed in the doorway. His presence filled the hallway. He seemed to stare right through her.

"Have you and Jim finished your discussion?" he asked.

"Yes," she said.

"Good. When you're ready, I'll see you downstairs," he said brusquely.

She nodded and hurried on to her room. Once there, Michelle relaxed in a tub of warm water, and forced herself to let go of all her tensions. She simply had to find a way to work with Rick without this wariness. She had prided herself on being a businesswoman. Yet, here she was, working on a difficult merger, and allowing herself to think about personal problems instead of behaving in a professional way.

Michelle took her time dressing, putting off the time when she would have to go downstairs. She knew that all the women would be looking her over carefully. She knew from experience that some of the women would be surprised by her youth. They would be expecting a much older woman. They would probably expect to see her dressed in a dark suit and uncomfortable shoes, with her hair pulled back in a severe fashion. She smiled in amusement.

So many times, she had seen that shocked look. The women would try not to show the surprise they felt when they first saw her.

Michelle pulled on her dress, a turquoise knit, which made her large blue-green eyes glow like emeralds. The dress molded to her bodice and slim waist, then fell in graceful folds about her legs. She wore high-heeled sandals. Years ago she had sold all the family jewelry. She wore the only jewelry she had kept, a simple pair of diamond ear studs, which had been her grandmother's, and a narrow gold bracelet set with sixteen diamonds, which had been a gift from her father on her sixteenth birthday. That had been such a special birthday, and such a special gift, that she couldn't bear to sell it. The jeweler had offered her a fabulous sum for the bracelet, but she had decided that she would rather do without lunches for a lifetime than part with her father's bracelet.

Michelle brushed her hair loose and applied her makeup. Inspecting herself in the mirror, she twirled, then opened her bedroom door and walked to the stairs.

Voices, laughter, glasses clinking, all the party sounds came from the dining room. Michelle paused in the doorway, admiring Trang's magic which had transformed the room. The huge banquet table had been moved along a bare wall and set with an ivory lace cloth, and dozens of various-sized candles twinkled invitingly. Adding to the warmth, a blazing fire crackled in the fireplace. The drapes at the French doors were drawn open to allow the last of the sun's rays to display the colorful banks of mums which grew in profusion on the terrace outside.

Mac was stationed behind the small bar, mixing drinks. He was dressed in a crisp white shirt with the sleeves rolled up above his elbows.

Trang, dressed in a somber, dark suit and white shirt, moved among the guests carrying a silver tray of appetizers. His face was wreathed in a smile as he accepted the compliments of the guests.

When Mac spotted Michelle, he walked from behind the bar and handed her a glass of wine.

"Wow!" he said. "You're gorgeous! The boss told me what you drink," he added, winking at her.

She smiled and thanked him, then turned to look over the guests in the room. Rick was at the far end of the dining room, talking earnestly with two men. His eyes scanned the room, stopping suddenly at Michelle. His eyes lingered on her, then he excused himself and started toward her. Before he reached her side, Jim Bannon stepped beside her and smiled.

"Michelle, you look beautiful," Jim said.

She accepted his compliment with a smile, and moved aside as Trang approached with a silver tray.

"You try, Missy," he urged. "You like."

"Umm. Smells delicious, Trang. What is it?" she asked.

Smiling broadly, he said, "Some seafood, some meat, Missy."

Michelle speared a round bite-sized portion and tasted it. It was bits of pork in a sweet sauce. From the other side of the tray, she tried the seafood.

"It's perfect, Trang," she said.

Rick had walked up to them, and was staring coolly at her.

Trang beamed as he offered the tray of food to his boss. "You try, Mr. Rick. Missy like them. You will too."

Rick grinned across at Michelle. Accepting the offering, he ate it and nodded.

"She's right, Trang. Perfect," he said.

Trang moved away, satisfied with the compliment.

"Jim," said Rick. "I'm going to introduce Mike around to the wives. Care to join us?" he asked.

"Sure thing," said Jim, moving along beside them.

Rick introduced Michelle and Jim to the wives. Nodding and smiling at the introductions, Michelle was aware of some curious glances by some of the women. Apparently, not all the wives had been made aware of her presence. One woman confessed that she had just assumed that Michelle was Jim's secretary. Jim and Michelle laughed at this admission. Then Michelle commented that it was a commonly made mistake.

"I hear that often," Michelle said, still chuckling.

A warm, deep woman's voice behind them made Michelle turn suddenly.

"Michelle! Burt told me how terrific you looked! I've been dying to see you!"

A tall, elegant woman, beautifully dressed in a black, silk cocktail-length gown, with her silver hair swept up in a sleek chignon, stood smiling at her. Michelle let out a little gasp, and the two women embraced.

"Anna! Oh, how good to see you!" she sighed.

Turning to Jim, Michelle said, "Anna, this is my boss, Jim Bannon. Jim, Anna Matheson, Burt's wife, and an old, dear friend," she added.

Taking her hand and leading her to a sofa, Anna sat next to Michelle and smiled. "Michelle. You look lovely. Tell me what you've been doing since I last saw you."

For nearly half an hour the two women sat comfortably, catching up on lost time. When Jim approached and asked Michelle to meet some more people, Michelle stood up reluctantly.

"We probably won't have much time to visit the rest of the evening, Anna. But it's been so good seeing you again. When we're back in Detroit, I'd like to phone you. Maybe we can arrange to get together for a really long visit."

"I'd like that, Michelle. Please call me," Anna said.

Then Michelle walked off with Jim Bannon to be introduced to some guests who had just arrived.

Rick invited his guests to feel free to inspect the downstairs rooms of the mansion. Most of the women eagerly began a tour. Rick was right, thought Michelle. The wives had been dying to look over this old place. They would have been very disappointed if they hadn't been invited to the castle tonight.

Rick led the women and a few of their husbands through the various rooms, keeping up a running commentary about the history of the house and the people who had once lived here. Michelle and Jim

Bannon, and several of the men stayed in the dining room, having already been in the rooms.

As the assembly reentered the dining room, one of the women asked, "Are you planning to sell this house, Mr. McCord?"

Michelle looked up and caught sight of Rick's strong profile as he turned toward the cluster of women.

"No. I won't sell it," he said.

"You mean you'd live in this big house all alone?" a second woman asked, flirting openly.

Michelle watched grimly as Rick charmed his group of admirers. "Well, I didn't say I'd be alone, did I?" he teased.

The women smiled knowingly among themselves. As Rick turned, he caught Michelle staring at him, and his lips turned up in a mocking smile. She quickly lowered her eyes.

By nine o'clock the guests were preparing to drive to the Harbor House for dinner. Trang, hovering near the door, accepting the praise of the guests, smiled warmly at everyone.

Mac was collecting half-finished drinks from the last of those guests who still remained.

As Michelle and Jim walked to the door, Rick called out, "Jim. There's no need to take two cars. Why don't you and Mike come with me?"

Jim accepted his invitation, and Michelle found herself walking between Jim and Rick toward the car.

As they rode along, Michelle said, "Well, Rick.

Do you think all the compliments tonight appeased Trang's anger?"

He chuckled. "Yes. He was certainly lapping up all that praise. Tomorrow, he'll be as happy as a kitten."

At the front door of the Harbor House Rick handed his keys to the parking attendant and preceded them into the room. Henri stood, waiting to greet his guests as they arrived. He warmly welcomed them, and escorted them to the dining room.

Michelle glanced around the room and felt a wave of nostalgia wash over her. There were so many happy memories here. She had always loved this room, with its cozy fireplace, its wall of windows overlooking the lake. She glanced beyond to the wide veranda, now bare of the wicker furniture used during the summer. She remembered again, hot summer nights, when the ladies in their chiffons sat waving fans, sipping cool drinks, while the gentlemen stood apart, talking business. The children would race around the wood railings, causing the women to occasionally look up and call sharply to them to stop their running.

Now Michelle looked up to see Rick staring at her. She composed herself and forced a smile.

"It all looks so familiar," she said softly.

"That's how I felt when I returned after so many years away," Rick said. "So many things I remembered about this place."

He put his hand under her elbow and led her toward a round table. Henri had set four large round tables in a circle. Each table was set for eight. They were covered with heavy, brown cloths, and wicker baskets filled with autumn foliage formed the centerpieces. Assorted large pumpkins stood guard near the fireplace. It was a warm, homey setting.

As the guests filed in, they found their seating arrangements by noting the name tags at each plate. Michelle found herself seated next to Rick at one table, while Jim was seated with Burt and Anna Matheson at another table.

During the exquisite dinner, Michelle found herself engaged in conversation with one of the men from Rick's legal staff. During a lull in the conversation, his wife suddenly asked, "Mrs. Scott. How is it that you have a job with so much responsibility at such a young age?"

Michelle smiled across the table at her and replied, "I guess because I had to become responsible at a young age."

Her husband picked up the thread of conversation and asked, "And what does your husband do, Mrs. Scott?"

Michelle thought she saw Rick start as his dark eyes flickered coldly over her. Though it was a question she often heard, she still found it a painful one to answer. She did not want to think about the gentle, ineffectual young lawyer whom she had married from compassion. It had been little enough to do for a dying man. Especially, as she had been sure that she would never be able to have the only man that she had or would ever love—Rick McCord, who was now scowling at her with such obvious contempt.

Before Michelle could pull herself together to frame a reply to the seemingly innocuous question, Rick had risen. Standing and lifting his glass, he said grandly, "Ladies and Gentlemen, may I have your attention for a moment, please. A toast to our gracious host, Henri LaRue."

So Rick had so little interest in her he did not even want to hear about the man she had married. So be it. It was probably better for both of them that he did not know that she was as free and as untouched as when she had first known him.

She smiled affectionately at Henri as he accepted the congratulations of the guests. Glasses raised, they toasted his hospitality. A piano player began to play dance tunes. The lights dimmed and several couples moved onto the floor to dance.

The guests at her table were dancing. Michelle and Rick were alone for a few minutes. She was staring at the couples dreamily swaying to the slow music, when she felt Rick's sudden movement. He was standing, holding his hand out to her.

"Dance?" he asked.

She placed her hand in his and allowed him to lead her to the dance floor. Rick fingered the delicate bracelet at her wrist, the diamonds twinkling, reflecting the candle lights.

"A gift from an admirer?" he asked.

"Yes," she replied.

When he waited for her explanation, she added, "My father. He gave it to me on my sixteenth birthday."

"It suits you," he murmured.

"Cold and hard like a diamond?" she quipped sarcastically.

His lips quirked in a hint of a smile. "I had more in mind sparkling and rare," he said quietly.

She bit her lip in annoyance. Why did she always have to be so defensive with Rick? Why couldn't she learn to keep her emotions under wraps?

As he drew her into his arms, she stiffened. Moving slowly to the music, Michelle felt her resolve slipping. She hated the weakness in herself that allowed Rick's touch to affect her this way.

Gradually, Michelle relaxed in Rick's arms, softly swaying to the music. He pulled her closer to him, and bent to whisper in her ear. She felt his warm breath on her temple, and moved her face up to reply. Their lips were almost touching. She stared into those compelling eyes, and saw herself reflected there.

She felt a heart beating. Was it his or hers? His arms felt so strong around her. Someone spoke as they danced by. Rick smiled, and Michelle felt his hand tighten its pressure on her back. She was drawn closer to him. Her hand, resting lightly on his shoulder, moved upward, her fingertips brushing the dark hair that curled above his collar.

She wanted the music to go on forever. To feel, for a little while longer, protected and safe in Rick's strong arms. She chanced a quick glance at his face. His eyes met hers, then moved down to linger on her mouth.

Self-consciously she moistened her lips. His hand tightened at her waist. He bent again and whispered, and Michelle felt a tiny shudder of pleasure.

When the music ended, Rick walked Michelle back to their table, his hand still resting against the small of her back. Her skin was warm where he touched her. There was a gentleness about his touch. He held her chair, then bent and excused himself, leaving her feeling suddenly cold and alone. He crossed the room and began speaking to Burt Matheson. Michelle forced herself not to watch him as he walked away. Instead, she glanced at Jim Bannon, dancing with Burt's wife, Anna. They were laughing together as they danced, and suddenly Michelle envied them their gaiety and laughter. If only she and Rick could relent and enjoy this beautiful evening. But they could never again relax and simply enjoy each other's company. They couldn't be easy and natural with each other. There was a chasm between them, and they could never bridge it.

Late into the night, Michelle danced with the men or chatted with their wives. She and Rick didn't dance together again, and they always seemed to be on opposite sides of the room. But several times, as she danced by or happened to glance up, she would see Rick's flinty eyes staring through her.

It was very late when the party finally broke up. Henri LaRue and Rick stood at the door bidding their guests good night. When the last couple had passed through the doorway, Rick glanced at Michelle and Jim, seated near the window, sipping coffee.

"Sorry I had to keep you up so late," he apologized.

"Nonsense," said Jim Bannon. "It's been a wonderful evening, Rick."

He glanced at Michelle for a confirmation, and she smiled warmly. "I've enjoyed it, Rick," she said simply.

"Well, if you two are ready, we can leave now," Rick offered.

They crossed the room and thanked Henri for the lovely evening. He accepted their praise graciously and took Michelle's hand.

"Michelle Miller," he said crisply. "You are still the most beautiful girl in the room."

"You always flattered me, Henri," she said laughing.

"We Frenchmen have an eye for beautiful women," he said, bending and kissing her on the cheek. "Good night, my dear. Sleep well."

"Thank you, Henri. Good night," she called as she followed Jim out the door.

Rick stayed behind to speak to Henri, and Michelle followed Jim to the car. They sat patiently until Rick came out and drove them home.

On the drive home the three of them fell silent. As they turned in at the opened iron gates and drove along the driveway toward the front door, Michelle thought it was like some crazy dream, sitting here next to Rick McCord, driving up to the old Winter Castle. But there was no joy being here with him. She felt stiff and uncomfortable. And tomorrow she would leave with Jim Bannon and go back to her job in Detroit, and Rick would go back to his office, wherever that was. They would go their separate ways, and this whole weekend would seem like just another cruel episode in her already shattered life.

As they walked up the stairs to their rooms, Jim patted her shoulder. "Michelle, you look all in. Get a good night's sleep," he said paternally.

She grinned at him. "Thanks, Dad."

At that he chuckled. "OK. I get your meaning. I'll stop sounding like the father figure. Good night, Michelle, Rick."

Rick and Michelle moved on without speaking until they reached Rick's door. She knew this door opened into a suite of rooms that old Mr. Winter had remodeled for his son and his bride when they first married. They had spent many happy summers here with him, until their accident. Afterward, the old man had moved back into this room, and had brought his young grandchild, Marla, to live with him in his castle.

And now, she thought sadly, Rick slept here.

He paused, his hand on the doorknob, and looked coldly at her. "Good night, Mike. Do you need anything?"

"Nothing. Good night," she whispered.

When she reached her door, Michelle pushed it open, then turned. Rick was still standing there, his hand on the opened door. She quickly walked into her room and closed her door, determined to shut out those eyes that seemed to stare through to her very soul.

Chapter Five

Upon awakening, Michelle moved about quickly. The room felt cold and damp as she scurried to the window. Drawing open the drapes, she realized that it must have stormed during the early morning, though it had not disturbed her sleep. Sodden piles of leaves and broken branches were strewn about the lawn. The sun was making a valiant effort to break through the clouds.

After a hot shower, Michelle pulled on heavy woolen slacks and a soft shirt. Carefully folding her clothes, she packed her suitcase, leaving out a warm jacket and scarf for the drive back to Detroit. She left her toilet articles in the bathroom. There would be time to pack them later.

Padding quietly down the stairs so as to not disturb

the others, Michelle glanced in the dining room. There was a place set at the table, but no one was about. She made her way to the kitchen. Trang looked up from the stove, smiling broadly. Michelle returned his smile, remembering what Rick had said the night before. Trang seemed pleased about the success of the cocktail party. He was happy as a kitten.

"Good morning, Trang. I see we had a storm," she remarked.

"Yes, Missy. Bad storm," he said. "This Michigan have funny weather. Different every day," he said, shaking his head.

"I take it I'm the first one up?" she asked.

"Oh, no, Missy. Mr. Rick up hours ago. He gone for a walk. Said he have a lot on his mind." Trang turned toward the cupboard. "You like coffee, Miss?" he asked.

"Yes, thank you. But nothing else just yet. It's too early to eat," she told him.

Accepting a steaming cup, she walked slowly back to the dining room. Stopping before the French doors, she watched the colorful patterns made by the sunlight through the stained-glass panes on either side of the doors. Pausing for a moment, she walked outside to the brick-paved courtyard beyond.

Colorful mums grew in every available inch of ground around the courtyard. Huge stone pots, some cracked or lying tipped on their sides, were planted with more mums and were set about among low bushes and evergreens.

From here, the lawn sloped down several hundred

yards to the lake. Giant willows stood almost at the water's edge, trailing their long wispy branches in the waves that lapped the shore. The sun was climbing higher above a bank of billowy clouds, casting golden fingers across the shimmering water.

Michelle drank in the sight of it all, wondering what it must be like to be greeted by this magnificent view every day. The small window of her cramped apartment in downtown Detroit looked out on a busy street, and her only view was the brick wall of the apartment building across the street. Not much to cheer the heart, she thought. But this!

Sighing, she turned to go back inside, then stopped abruptly. Rick was standing in the opened doorway. She had no idea how long he had been watching her.

"Good morning," she said as she approached him. "It's a fantastic view."

Rick moved aside for her to enter, and she brushed his arm as she walked by. The mere touch of him burned her skin.

Smiling at him, she added, "I was thinking how lucky you are to be able to enjoy such a spectacular sunrise whenever you choose."

"Still the romantic, I see," he said dryly, as he followed her to the table.

Before she could reply, Trang entered, carrying a heaping serving tray. Michelle noticed that a second place had been set at the table. Trang began spooning the food onto both plates.

"Oh, Trang," she said, smiling. "You forgot. I'm not eating."

Trang looked up at her. "Yes you are, Missy. Mr. Rick say to make you a big breakfast, like his."

She glanced in surprise at Rick. "But why, for heaven's sake?"

"You're too thin," he remarked casually. "I don't think you bother to eat."

"Oh!" One eyebrow arched ominously. "I'm too thin, am I? Well, what business is that of yours anyway!"

She struck a familiar pose, her hands on her hips, her chin jutting out defiantly.

Although Rick was frowning, his voice rumbled with laughter. He held her chair and said, "I see I've just lit the fuse again, Mike."

He touched her arm and indicated the chair. "Just keep me company while I eat, then." As she began to protest, he gently pressed his hands on her shoulders. "Please, for my sake."

Relenting, she sat down, her frown turning into a smile. As she tasted the eggs, she said gently, "I have to admit. It's a tempting breakfast."

While they ate, Trang bustled in and out of the dining room, returning with orange juice and refilling their coffee cups.

"How do you like working at Forest, Mike?" Rick asked her.

"I like it," she replied automatically.

His look held her. "I mean, how do you really like it?" he said firmly.

"And I mean I really like it!" she tossed back. She paused a moment, then added, "I like the people I work with. And I like accomplishing something. Haven't you been listening to Jim Bannon? I'm good, Rick."

At his surprised look, she laughed lightly. "Does that sound conceited to you?" She tossed her head, and although she laughed again, her voice took on an edge. "I guess it is hard to imagine, but I do manage to turn out a respectable amount of work at Forest. And I'm good at what I do."

Then, aware of Rick's watchful gaze and the intensity of her own words, Michelle ducked her head and avoided his eyes.

"I know what you're thinking, Rick. That I'm one of the spoiled little rich kids. Isn't that what you once said?"

"I don't remember including you in that category, Mike," he said softly.

"It doesn't matter. I could see your surprise at my statements just now. You find it amazing that someone from your side of town can work. Well, you aren't the only one who had to learn how." She watched him over the rim of her cup.

"OK. You're right, Mike. I guess I do find it a little hard to swallow. Listening to Jim Bannon rave about his wonderful little assistant. And reading the reports you've prepared for our organization. It's hard to credit you with all that. Or maybe I've just been trying to find a flaw in it all." He raised one eyebrow. "Just for the record," he said quietly, "you've done your job well."

Before she could respond, Jim Bannon walked in.

"Good morning," he greeted them. "What a relaxing place this is." He turned to Rick. "It's so quiet here. No traffic sounds. No sirens in the night. I don't think I've slept this well in years."

He sat down, and almost instantly Trang was serving his breakfast. Michelle and Rick enjoyed second cups of coffee while Jim ate.

When he was finished, Rick said, "I've called a brief meeting at noon. I know everyone wants to get on the road fairly early. We ought to be able to wrap it up within an hour or two."

"That's fine," said Jim, winking at Michelle.

She relaxed. Things had gone more smoothly than she would have believed. Rick obviously hadn't been thrilled to see her, but he hadn't been difficult to work with. And she had feared that some of his associates might resent working with a woman, but her fears had proved groundless. In just a few hours she would be on the way home. And in no time, this whole weekend would seem like just a brief interlude. Perhaps, in time, she would even be able to put it out of her mind entirely. She should be overjoyed, but a feeling of depression swept over her.

"If you two will excuse me," Michelle stood up. "I'll go upstairs and finish packing."

In her room she packed away the last of her articles. Then, with so little time left, Michelle stood at the tall windows in her room and allowed herself to stare lovingly at the grounds below.

A light tap on her door brought her back to reality.

Jim's voice called, "Michelle. The others are

arriving for the meeting. We'll be down in the library."

"OK, Jim. Thanks. I'll be right there," she called.

She ran a comb through her coppery hair and headed for the meeting downstairs.

As she entered the library, Michelle noticed that for the first time Rick was seated at his desk, with his entire staff assembled at a long table which had been apparently set up just for this meeting. Jim Bannon was seated at the far end of the table. Michelle smiled apprehensively at the assembly and took a seat next to Jim.

Mac appeared, dressed in a crisp shirt and tie, and began passing out typewritten pages to everyone. Michelle realized suddenly that Mac was not a handyman about the place, but more probably Rick's secretary. She smiled as this realization dawned on her. She would have pictured Rick with a beautiful, stylish woman in his office, not this obliging young man.

Mac took a seat at a small table slightly behind Rick and spread open his notebook. As the meeting began, Mac took notes.

Most of the points being discussed today were legal, and Burt Matheson and his staff did most of the talking. Within an hour, almost on cue, the men assembled around the table seemed to have concluded their discussion.

Michelle glanced at Jim, to see if he had anything more to add.

"Well, gentlemen. Have we answered everything to your satisfaction?" Jim asked.

Michelle saw Burt's eyes meet Rick's. There was an almost imperceptible nod of his head, and then Burt spoke.

"So far, everything seems most satisfactory. If we are all in agreement, then . . ." Burt looked around the table and smiled. "We will expect to conclude negotiations in a few weeks. In the meantime . . ." He looked directly at Michelle. "Mrs. Scott can stay on here and work out the details with Mr. McCord. As soon as they feel satisfied that everything is in order, we will all meet back here to conclude our merger."

Michelle sat in stunned silence. She couldn't believe what Burt had just said. She looked at Rick. The look he returned was bland. But she felt certain that behind that impassive look, he was laughing at her. This had to be a direct order from Rick. Even though Burt acted as the spokesman, she felt certain that all of this had been orchestrated by Rick McCord.

Realizing that Jim Bannon was speaking, Michelle turned to him abruptly.

."Of course, if you think it can be concluded that quickly, we'd be delighted to oblige." Jim looked at her and smiled. "You realize we weren't prepared for this. I'm sure Mrs. Scott brought very little with her."

She nodded, hoping they might see the inconvenience they were causing. Burt merely nodded, and said, "Yes, of course. But, Michelle, since you will be doing your work here at the house, you won't need proper office attire. And there is a very well-equipped laundry in the basement. If there's anything you really need from your home, I'll be flying in from time to time. I'd be more than happy to pick up anything you want."

Michelle felt trapped. Glancing at Jim, she saw the question in his eyes. She knew how desperately he wanted this merger. And she knew that, no matter how she felt, she couldn't let him down. She compressed her lips together in an effort to control her anger.

So, she thought, *this is what Rick was mulling over in his mind early this morning while he tramped through the woods! How to trap me! And all the while, at breakfast, he was charming me, filling my head with flattery. Telling me what a good job I had done! What a petty, vindictive thing to do!*

He knew she couldn't refuse to stay here. Not with Jim Bannon pinning all his hopes on her. Not with all these business associates of Rick's sitting around the table watching her reaction.

She fought down the fury rising in her throat. Gritting her teeth, she realized that Rick had the upper hand. There wasn't a thing she could do to get out of this. And he had known it all along.

Then, staring around the table, Michelle said as calmly as possible, "Well, of course this is unexpected. But it is what we've all been working for, isn't it?"

She forced herself to look at Rick, and she felt his eyes mocking her. How cool he looked! And how she would love to refuse, just to wipe that smug look from his face. But, of course, she wouldn't. She would never let Jim down, and Rick had counted on this.

The men were standing, snapping shut their attaché cases and shrugging into coats. Michelle and Jim stood at the door, shaking hands with Rick's staff, thanking them for their consideration. Michelle felt Rick moving to her side, but she continued to rivet her attention on the men who were leaving. She felt as though her face would crack if she had to continue to smile much longer. Finally, only Burt and his assistant were left.

Burt took her proffered hand in both of his and smiled apologetically. "Michelle. I realize this decision caught you off-guard," he murmured.

"It's all right, Burt. I understand. You were only doing your job," she said quietly.

"Thank you, dear. I'm glad you understand." He smiled, squeezing her hands.

"Be sure you give my love to Anna," Michelle told him. "And tell her I'll remember to phone her when I'm back home. It was so good to see her again. I've missed her . . . missed you both." Michelle stood on tip-toe to kiss Burt quickly on the cheek. He returned the kiss, then walked away.

Michelle said her goodbyes to the others and headed for the stairs. At the top of the steps, Jim Bannon caught up with her.

"Well," he said, smiling broadly. "What did I tell you! You really impressed those guys, Michelle. Can you believe it! Inside of one little weekend, you've got this whole merger moving toward completion.

Honey, this is just about the best thing that's ever happened!"

With that, he hugged her, then held her a little away from him. Staring at her strained expression, he hesitated. "Michelle. It is all right, isn't it? I mean, you don't mind staying on and getting this whole thing over with, do you?"

Michelle felt ashamed of herself. Jim was so excited, and she couldn't bring herself to share his enthusiasm. Forcing a brightness she didn't feel, she said, "Jim. Of course I'm happy about it. It's what we wanted. It's just—I wasn't expecting to stay here. I thought I'd be doing the work at our office. I'm just—overwhelmed, I guess."

Jim patted her shoulder comfortingly. "Sure, I understand, Michelle. But this sure beats an office for working, doesn't it?"

She smiled determinedly at him. "I may have a hard time settling back down to our old office after a few weeks of this."

But her mind was already whirling. How could she possibly work here, knowing that she and Rick were in the same house, eating their meals together, sleeping just a room apart?

Jim walked into his room and returned with his suitcase. "Want to walk me down to the car?" he asked.

"Sure," she replied, and they walked down the stairs together, and outside into the chill autumn afternoon.

Jim tossed his suitcase into the trunk, then took

off his suit jacket and draped it over the seat. He rolled back the cuffs of his shirt, then casually dropped his arm across Michelle's shoulders.

"Now remember, Michelle. If there's anything you need, give me a call. Burt Matheson repeated his offer. He'll be flying in here a couple of times, and he'd be more than happy to bring along anything you ask for. Just phone, and I'll send one of the girls from the office to your apartment." He smiled down at her. "If all goes well, I guess I'll be seeing you in a few weeks. Take care."

He patted her shoulder affectionately and then settled himself comfortably in his sports car. After starting the engine, Jim looked beyond Michelle to smile and wave. She guessed without turning around that Rick was walking toward her. He must have politely waited until Jim and Michelle had said their goodbyes, she thought.

With a casual wave of his hand, Jim Bannon drove off. At the end of the long driveway, he turned the car onto the road and roared away.

Michelle shivered in the chill air, and Rick's arm was suddenly around her shoulders, steering her toward the house.

"You're freezing," he said angrily.

"I didn't realize it was this cold outside. I didn't wear my jacket," she said, suddenly feeling foolish.

His arm was still around her shoulders, urging her toward the library. There, he led her to the sofa, pulled up before the fireplace. A log fire crackled invitingly. Michelle was grateful for its heat. She sat for some time, hugging her arms about herself, feeling the warmth spreading through her.

Rick left the room, returning a short time later with a tray loaded with a steaming pot of coffee, mugs, cream and sugar. He handed her a mug of coffee and poured himself one as well.

"Um. Thanks," she said. "This fire feels wonderful." She sipped her coffee in silence.

Rick stood, one foot on the raised hearth, drinking his coffee and regarding her.

"I hope you have warmer clothes than those," he said thoughtfully.

"One sweater, one jacket. That's all I brought," she said weakly.

"I'll look around and see what I have here," he said. "My stuff will be way too big for you, but at least it will be warm," he added.

"I can manage with the sweater and jacket," she said coldly.

Now that she was warm again, she was remembering why she was here. Rick had been the one who had engineered this whole thing. He had sprung this trap on her. She didn't know why yet, but she was sure he would let her know in his own sweet time.

Noticing the edge to her voice, Rick smiled lazily.

"I see you're feeling like your old self again." He set the empty mug on the tray and walked to his desk.

"Dinner will be around six o'clock," he said, as though dismissing her.

Michelle turned on him, no longer able to control

the explosion of fury that had been building within her.

"You've deliberately kept me here! This wasn't Burt's idea, even though you made it look that way. I'm well aware that Burt takes his orders from you. Why, Rick? Why in the world would you want to keep me here, when we both know you can't stand to even look at me? Do you want to punish me? Is that it? Wouldn't we both be better off if we could forget the past? Bury it?"

He moved from the desk and came across the room so quickly that Michelle had no time to react. He took her roughly by the shoulders. Staring down at her, he hissed, "Still the little spitfire, aren't you!" His eyes raked over her red hair, the sparks flying from her blue-green eyes. "Some of that tomboy is still there, Mike. You try to keep her hidden under that sophisticated look you've affected. But once in a while she breaks loose."

His lips turned up in a hint of a smile. His fingers absently stroked a silken strand of her hair. Very softly, he said, "And you're wrong on another score, Mike. I do like looking at you. I like it very much."

Michelle tore herself from his hands and strode to the door. Turning, she flung him a hate-filled look and spit out her words carelessly.

"When I realized you were Mico Industries, and that I would have to work with you, I promised myself that for Jim Bannon's sake, and for the sake of old Joe Forest's memory, I'd find a way to manage. But I was wrong, Rick. There's no way I can stay here and work this out. If you'll just get me transportation back to Detroit, I'll train someone to handle this merger as quickly as possible."

Her hand on the doorknob, she froze as she heard his words. "No, Mike. No running away. You'll stay and work this out. If you really care about your boss, Jim Bannon, as you say you do, and all the others who work at Forest Corporation, you'll stay here as long as I say. And you'll find a way to work with me."

Michelle turned and faced him.

"And if I have to spell it out for you, Mike," he added, "I will. You said it yourself. I am Mico Industries. I make the decisions. And the board agrees with those decisions. If I decide that I'm no longer interested in a merger, then the deal is off."

Michelle opened her mouth to protest, but Rick cut her off.

"Jim Bannon had a lot of flattering things to say about you. He seems to think you can do anything you set your mind to. Well, I'm not Jim Bannon," he said comtemptuously. "You'll have to show me a lot more than I've seen this weekend. Before I'm through, I intend to know Forest Corporation inside and out. I want a complete picture of their finances, their inventory, and especially their talent pool. I want to know every employee, and how much he can do. I want an expert opinion, Mike. Bannon seems to think you're that expert." Rick's eyes glittered dangerously. "Well, I'll be the judge of that."

He moved to within inches of her, towering above her. "You said you care about old Joe Forest's memory. Well, Mike, be warned. If Forest Corporation fails, that's all you and the other employees will have left—a memory. Forest Corporation can't survive without this merger. You and I both know it. They'll cave in without immediate financial support."

Rick turned toward his desk. "So, don't talk to me about running home to train someone else to take your place here. We both know there isn't time for that."

His voice lowered angrily. "And I'm not buying that story anyway. We both know why you don't want to stay and work with me. But you'll manage. You have no choice."

She could feel the venom in his voice. She felt as though there were ice in her veins.

Then, as calmly as though he were talking about the weather, he added, "Better get some rest. We have a lot of work to do in the next few weeks."

She tore open the door and fled upstairs to her room.

Chapter Six

Alone in her room, Michelle unpacked her suitcase and carefully hung her clothes in the closet. After laying out her toilet articles in the bathroom and stowing the empty suitcase on the floor of the closet, she began to pace the room. There were hours to kill before dressing for dinner. She couldn't simply hide here in her room.

She stopped before a glass shelf crammed with dusty sculptures. Rolling up her sleeves, she filled the bathroom sink with soapy water, then began washing each figurine before replacing it on the shelf. Each sculpture was an exquisite horse in a different pose. Surely they had been Marla Winter's collection. Michelle wondered why Marla had allowed them to remain here.

When that was finished, Michelle moved about

the room, dusting the furniture, shaking the curtains and drapes. With a little work, she thought, this room could be quite elegant again.

By the time Michelle had finished cleaning the room, she realized with satisfaction that she had managed to fill several hours. Now, she stripped off her dusty clothes and soaked in the tub. She washed her hair and, wrapping a towel around herself, proceeded to blow-dry her hair. She repaired her chipped nail polish and dressed for dinner.

The green silk dress and jade jacket seemed too dressy for a casual dinner, but she had brought so little with her, she had no choice. Applying her makeup, Michelle stared at herself in the mirror. *If you can do just one thing tonight,* she told herself, *it is this. Control that temper!*

Grinning, she gave one last glance at her reflection in the mirror, then snapped off the light and walked down the stairs.

Glancing in the dining room, Michelle was surprised to see the room in darkness. She switched on the light, and saw that the table wasn't set for dinner. Puzzled, she turned off the light and walked down the hall to the kitchen. Trang was bent over the oven, checking something inside. He glanced up quickly, then smiled at Michelle.

"You look for Mr. Rick?" he asked in his slight sing-song voice.

Trang seemed to be in extremely good humor. He had tied a white apron about his waist, his sleeves rolled up to his elbows. He smiled broadly.

"Yes. Are we eating in here?" she asked.

"Oh, no. In Mr. Rick's library. You go ahead, Missy. I bring dinner when it ready," he said.

"Is Mac in there too?" she asked, fervently hoping for some company.

"No. Mac upstairs, dressing," Trang told her.

"Oh good. He's joining us for dinner?" she asked, feeling relieved.

"No. We eat in town. Mac driving me to town for movie later," Trang explained.

Michelle sighed. She had counted on having someone around to keep the conversation going. She dreaded being alone with Rick all evening. Frowning, she left the kitchen and walked to the library.

The door was open, and she could see Rick at his desk, bent over some papers. As she walked in, he continued to write for several moments before he looked up.

His eyes raked over her coldly, then he shuffled the papers and set them aside.

"Since Trang and Mac are going to town, I thought it would be silly for just the two of us to eat in the dining room. It's too big and formal," he said.

"Yes. This is fine," she assured him, not wanting to annoy him. She must remember to be pleasant. Pleasant and agreeable.

"Would you like a drink?" he asked.

"Um, if you're having one," she said.

He raised one eyebrow, but made no comment. Walking to a cabinet, he expertly made his drink, then poured her a glass of wine.

As he handed her the long-stemmed glass, he commented, "You didn't have to dress for dinner, Mike."

She glanced at him, then looked him up and down. He was wearing black pants and a soft blue silk shirt. Not exactly old working clothes. He saw her look of amusement.

"Well," he confessed, "I did clean up a little. But not exactly formal, you'll admit."

"I really had no choice, Rick. I didn't bring much with me. Remember?" she added casually.

He nodded. As he walked to the fireplace, he said almost inaudibly, "You look beautiful, Mike."

Surprised at his unexpected compliment, she said, "Thank you."

There was an awkward silence.

When Trang entered carrying a huge tray, they both were grateful for the distraction.

A small round table had been set up across the room, near the fireplace. It was covered with a heavy damask cloth, and fine china and silver. A low bowl of gardenias gave off their heavily perfumed scent. Michelle found herself wondering where Trang could have possibly found gardenias at this time of the year.

While Trang placed the steaming dishes on the table, Rick carried two chairs over. On a coffee table, Trang set up a tray with coffee and dessert. He lit several candles in glass containers.

Hovering about, he asked, "Is this everything you need, Mr. Rick?"

Rick nodded. "Everything's fine, Trang. I know

you're eager to get to the movie. If we need anything, we can find it in the kitchen. Thanks."

Trang smiled at them both, dimmed the lights and left the room.

Rick looked down at Michelle as he held her chair for her. After the first few uncomfortable moments, they both began to relax and enjoy Trang's excellent dinner.

Afterward, sipping her drink, Michelle asked timidly, "Rick. How did you happen to buy the Winter Castle?"

"I heard it was for sale. I made an offer. They accepted. That was all," he said noncommittally.

"But how could Marla Winter bear to part with it?" she asked.

"I thought you knew. I'm sure it was in all the papers. Marla Winter is dead," he said.

"Dead! No, I never heard. How did she die, Rick?" Michelle was now alert.

Rick swirled the amber liquid in his glass and stared into it thoughtfully.

"I take it you haven't been brought up to date on the Winters. Marla died here in Harbor Springs." He looked up at Michelle. "From what I've heard, little Marla was pretty used to having her own way. Her dear old grandfather had always given her everything she ever wanted. He even gave her things she didn't think of having. I don't think that old guy ever said no to her. Until she wanted an Italian count."

"An Italian count!" Michelle smiled. "I remember hearing rumors of a count chasing her."

Rick added, "Marla was in school in Europe. I don't know how old Jacob Winter managed to let her out of his sight. She must have been pretty pursuasive to talk him into letting her go away to school. Anyway, before the first year was over, she was making headlines by being pursued all over the Continent by an Italian playboy. The old man saw the pictures in all the papers, of course. But I think he was pretty sure Marla would get tired of this one like she got tired of all the rest. Then, one Christmas, she flew home with the Count to ask her grandfather's permission to marry. Naturally, Jacob Winter had already had the Count investigated pretty thoroughly. From what he had learned, he absolutely refused to allow the marriage."

Rick walked to the fireplace and turned to face Michelle.

"Can you imagine Marla's reaction when her grandfather refused her! I guess she flew into a rage. She threatened to never see him again if he didn't change his mind. I suppose the old man really thought she would stew for a while and then get over it. But he forgot one thing. Marla had always had everything she ever wanted. And she wanted the Count. She took off for Europe and refused to come home. I think Marla figured her grandfather would have to accept him. But she wasn't counting on all the complications."

"What happened?" asked Michelle eagerly.

"Well, for one thing, the Count was already married. And his wife, being a devout Catholic, refused to consider a divorce. Marla was a very determined young woman. She pursuaded the Count to fly with her to Haiti. There, he obtained a quickie divorce and married Marla. But his divorce wasn't recognized as valid in Italy. That made his marriage to Marla a bigamous relationship. He very quickly decided that he didn't love Marla enough to give up his home and all his possessions in Italy. So, in a matter of months, he left her and went back to his wife."

"And Marla. What happened to her?" asked Michelle.

"It pretty much destroyed her," said Rick. "When he left her, she was too proud to admit defeat and come back to her grandfather. I heard she just drifted around Europe, staying with friends, partying a lot and trying to keep up a pretense of indifference. There were too many lovers, and too much drinking. It finally all caught up with her. But still she wouldn't come home. She was a regular guest at all the glittering parties. But the gaiety was a little forced. When the old man finally died, all alone, she came home to bury him. It was the first time she had set foot in this house since that Christmas she came home with the Count. After the funeral, Marla came back here alone. From what the police could put together, she just drank herself into a stupor, then climbed into her sports car and tore up the highway."

Michelle shivered and walked to the fireplace. Staring into the flames, she asked, "Who got the house?"

"A bunch of distant relatives," Rick said. "They

were approached by a developer to sell. He wanted to section off the land and build a modern subdivision around the lake. He offered them a good price. When I heard about it, I made them a better offer."

Michelle turned and stared at him. "Why?"

He shrugged. "I wanted to."

A sudden awkward silence stretched between them.

Michelle shook her head sadly. "Poor Marla. How could she have waited all those years, knowing her grandfather was so lonely. He loved her so much."

Rick's eyes were bleak. "People always seem to hurt the ones who love them. It's a fact of life, Mike."

"Oh Rick. That sweet old man! She was his whole life!" she whispered.

His eyes blazed across the space between them, burning into hers. "Why should you care? What are they to you anyway?" he snapped.

"Nothing, I suppose. Just part of my childhood here. It was such a romantic story. The rich old man who treasured his only grandchild. I thought she was so beautiful, so . . . glamorous."

Rick caught her arm, and his eyes glittered. "But in reality, he was a foolish old man, and she was a narrow, selfish witch."

Michelle's temper flared. "You and I see things so differently. Your reality and mine are completely opposite. The truth probably lies somewhere in between. But they were both tragic figures, caught up in something they couldn't control."

Now Rick's smile mocked her.

As she pulled her arm roughly away from him, he caught both her arms in his hands, painfully gripping the soft flesh.

"Your reality and mine are more than just different, Mike! They're light-years apart," he said. "Tragic figures!" he muttered sarcastically. "The fact is, he should have found something else to fill his life besides a beautiful butterfly who only knew how to take and not to give. And she should have realized that she couldn't go through life comparing every man she met with that doting grandfather, who was perfectly content to give her every little thing she ever wanted."

Michelle tried to twist her arms from his grasp, but this only made him tighten his grip.

"They weren't tragic, Mike. They were complete fools!" he hissed.

"I don't think we're talking about the Winters now, Rick," she whispered.

They stared at each other. Neither moved. In the black pools of his eyes, Michelle saw herself reflected. Her pulse was hammering in her temple. She felt suddenly afraid. If she didn't turn and run, now, before she betrayed her emotions, she would be lost. She twisted in his grip, attempting to break free.

Without any warning, Rick pulled Michelle roughly into his arms and brought his lips down hard on hers. It happened so quickly. Michelle stiffened, hoping to push him away. Her hands were against his chest, pushing ineffectively at him. His strong arms pulled her tighter against his hard body.

Standing perfectly still, she stopped fighting him. He raised his head and looked down at her. Her lips felt bruised from his punishing kiss. She turned her head to avoid his eyes.

It seemed to Michelle that everything after that happened in slow motion. Rick's hand caught her chin, and tilted her face up to his. He brushed his fingers lightly across her lips, murmuring, "Mike."

She lowered her long lashes, veiling her eyes. Then, her eyes opened wide and she stared at him with such longing, she knew he could read the desire in them. His face descended so slowly toward hers, she thought he would never reach her lips. Standing on tip-toe, she raised her face to his. As he began to kiss her, she brought her hands up, encircling his neck. He parted her lips and his tongue plundered the sweetness of her mouth. Just as she thought her breath would choke in her throat, he dragged his lips across her cheek and kissed the sensitive area beneath her ear. Shuddering, she molded her body tightly to his, feeling the hard length of his thigh against hers. Rick brought his lips to the hollow of her throat, moving his hands sensuously down her body to press her hips closer to him. She felt as though caught on a tide of passion so powerful she could not break its hold. In an attempt to stop his kisses, she brought her hand up to his mouth. He caught hold of it and buried his lips in her palm. She caught her breath, then felt her limbs begin to melt.

She brought her hands up around his neck, twisting her fingers in the thick, dark hair.

"Oh, Rick!" It was a half-sob, catching in her throat. Her breathing was ragged.

He caught her shoulders and held her slightly away from him. His eyes were glazed, smoldering with fire. His face darkened with a puzzled frown.

"You're supposed to say, 'You shouldn't have kissed me like that,'" he whispered.

Michelle felt the sudden flame of humiliation burn her cheeks.

"All right. I'll say it for you. I had no right to do that. I guess I forgot for a moment this wasn't yesterday. It's today. But old habits die hard, Mike."

He stared down at the still trembling figure in his arms.

"I don't get it, Mike. You've only been away from home a couple of days. Certainly not long enough to be this hungry. Doesn't that husband of yours satisfy you?" His eyes narrowed as he added, "And while you're here in Harbor Springs with me, Mrs. Scott, what do you suppose Mr. Scott will be doing?"

It was as though he had slapped her!"

She stared at him in horror. Bitter tears stung her eyelids. She flashed him a hard, glittering look before turning abruptly from him. How dare he say such cruel things! How could she explain David to Rick? Gentle, sweet David. How she treasured his memory. She brushed the tears from her cheeks. Then, suddenly, a wave of fury swept over her.

Turning to face Rick, her eyes blazing, she

shouted, "Don't mention my husband, Rick! Not ever! You're not fit to mention his name!"

Then she fled, sobbing as though her heart would break.

For a long while after she left the room, Rick stood lost in thought, staring at the flames in the fireplace.

Chapter Seven

Michelle awoke with a start. A glance at the clock on her night table told her that it was early. She padded to the window and threw open the drapes. Heavy frost glittered on the lawn below, a grim reminder that winter came early in this North country. One morning she could wake to see a dusting of snow on the ground.

She shivered. She wasn't ready for winter. Wasn't ready for Rick either, waiting downstairs to begin another round.

Showering quickly, Michelle wrapped herself in a thick bath sheet and sat down to dry her hair. As she worked the hair blower over the wet strands of hair, she stared at the portrait of Marla Winter over the bed. But it wasn't Marla that Michelle was thinking about. It was the ugly scene with Rick last night.

The way her resolve had weakened the minute he touched her was proof enough to Michelle that she couldn't pretend she didn't feel anything for Rick. It would be disastrous to ever again let him get close to her or kiss her like that. But last night's scene had given her a weapon against Rick's control of her emotions. He wasn't aware that she was a widow. She must never let him know the truth. If they were to maintain a working relationship, Michelle must keep Rick at bay.

She thought again of what Connie had said so many years ago. "Rick McCord can have any girl he wants."

Well, Michelle thought angrily, *I'm sure he's still stung by my father's crimes against his father. And if he thinks he can use me, then toss me aside, I'll use all the weapons at my disposal to fight him. I can't let him see what effect he really has on me.*

Michelle twisted the wedding band on her finger. David's ring. She thought about David Scott, the young man whose name she still bore. Although their marriage had never been consummated, she had vowed she would always remember him lovingly.

Last night, Rick had wondered aloud why she had responded so readily to his advances. It would be better if he continued to think that she simply got carried away in a moment of weakness. If he ever knew that she had never loved any man except him, he would take advantage of her inexperience.

As she studied her reflection in the mirror, she reminded herself that she must manage to handle this situation with as much dignity as she could. She would do her job, and then get on with her life. And she must leave here with no regrets. And no humiliation. This town had witnessed one scandal in the Miller family. She wouldn't add to the record. She must keep Rick at a distance until her work here was finished.

Michelle dressed in warm woolen slacks and a sweater, the creamy beige color contrasting with her bright turquoise eyes and the pinpoints of color on her cheeks.

She brushed her shining hair loose and, giving a last glance at the smiling girl in the portrait, she closed her door and walked downstairs.

Michelle moved quickly past the dining room, without a glance to see if Rick might be there. She hurried on to the kitchen. Trang looked up from the stove. Mac was eating at the kitchen table.

"Good morning," Mac called.

Trang turned and gave his imitation of a smile. "Good morning, Missy. You like coffee?"

She smiled at them both. "Yes. Please. And if you don't mind, Mac, I'll join you for breakfast in here."

He grinned at her. "I see you've discovered the boss's rotten mood this morning too," he said.

"Oh." She lifted her head. "Is Rick in bad humor?"

"Bad humor!" Mac smiled knowingly at Trang. "We both got out of his way fast."

As Michelle sat down at the table, Trang began setting a place for her.

"How you like your eggs, Missy?" he asked.

"Oh, no eggs, Trang. Just toast. I can't eat when I first get up in the morning." She smiled across the table at Mac. "I haven't seen Rick yet this morning. I wonder if he'll want to work, if he's as angry as you say."

"There's no way of knowing until he tells me," Mac answered. "But I don't mind if he takes the day off. I've still got a lot of paperwork to take care of."

Trang set a plate of toast in front of Michelle, then poured himself a cup of coffee.

"How long have you been here in Michigan?" she asked them both.

Mac answered, "Oh, a couple of weeks." He glanced at Trang, who nodded his assent. "One day, out of the blue, Rick said we were flying to Michigan. We spent a day here while he signed the papers and directed the workmen to make some changes in a few outbuildings, then we flew on to Detroit. We spent another day there. I don't know what the boss was doing there. He never called for me. I think he spent the entire day in his hotel room. Anyway, the next day, we were back in Florida, where he had a project going. We didn't see this place again until a few weeks ago, when we moved in. Judging by the condition of this old house, the boss hasn't even bothered to contact any workmen about remodeling it. Maybe he doesn't intend to spend enough time here to bother with remodeling."

He shrugged. "I haven't heard him say what he intends to do with all this."

Michelle felt a sadness come over her while Mac spoke. Why had Rick bought this mansion, if he didn't care enough to make repairs or live here? Maybe her original thought about this place was correct. It was just purchased as an investment. Another of Rick's money-making projects.

She roused herself from her thoughts as she heard Trang say, "I never see Mr. Rick so on edge. He seem to have too much on his mind. You know what bother him, Missy?"

As Trang and Mac both glanced expectantly at Michelle, she felt herself flush. Shrugging, she stammered, "I can't imagine. You both know him better than I."

Mac said, "I got the impression you and Rick were old friends."

Mac seemed to be regarding her closely. Michelle shifted nervously. "Well, yes," she hedged. "We are old friends. But it's been years since I last saw Rick. I'm afraid I don't know him very well anymore."

Michelle was reluctant to answer any questions about herself and her earlier years here. That could lead to all kinds of embarrassing questions. Instead, she was determined to keep Mac and Trang from probing any further into her life.

She quickly changed the subject. "Do you type, Mac?" she asked innocently.

"Sure do," he replied. "I suppose that's how I got into this secretarial work," he said, smiling.

"Oh? How do you mean?" Michelle asked, cupping her chin in her hands. "I've been wondering how you happened to get the job as Rick's secretary."

"I started out planning to be an accountant," Mac

began. "I just happened to fall into secretarial work," he said. "I discovered I had a natural talent for this sort of thing. In college, I found out that I could make a lot of money by typing papers for my friends. A lot of the guys had handwriting that was so sloppy the instructors couldn't read their papers. When they found out that I'd type them for a small fee, I was in business."

Mac smiled, remembering. "It's funny. I found out that I liked the work. Just for kicks, I took a shorthand course. I was the only guy in the class." He chuckled. "I only took the course because I liked a girl who was taking that course, and I wanted to be near her."

Michelle smiled across the table at Mac. His sandy-colored hair and smiling, freckled countenance would charm any girl. His blue eyes danced with a laughter that was always bubbling just below the surface. Mac was the sort of charmer who would make it impossible to stay angry. His good humor was contagious.

Trang turned from the stove and grinned. "Same old story with Mac, Missy Scott. Always a girl."

Michelle laughed, and Mac shrugged his shoulders. "Why not? She was the prettiest girl on campus. And I found out in a few weeks that I was better at shorthand than she was. In no time, I was helping her with her homework."

Turning to wink at Michelle, he added, "And from that humble beginning, a secretary was born."

Michelle smiled. "And did you get the girl, Mac?"

He grinned good-naturedly. "No. Wouldn't you

know, she fell for a big football player who couldn't even spell."

They all burst out laughing.

"Mac," Michelle asked. "How do you like working for Rick?"

"He's the greatest," Mac said, serious for a moment. "He's fair, and decent, and completely honest. Also," and a smile spread slowly across his mouth, "I get to travel and see the world. Rick has his own plane and pilot."

Michelle was surprised at this. "Really? And does he need his own plane? I mean, does he need to do that much traveling?" she asked.

"He sure does," Mac replied. "I guess we've been practically all over the world."

Trang nodded. Then he added, "Mr. Rick get restless, after a while. Then, without warning, we pack up and move on."

Michelle felt crushed. This was just a temporary stop for Rick. He would stay a few weeks or months, while the merger was being arranged. Then, on to some other place.

Rick had been strangely quiet that day he had told her there was no wife. Was he implying that a wife would be in the way? Yes, she thought. Having a wife would cramp his style. Connie's words taunted her. "Old love 'em and leave 'em Rick McCord."

When the spirit moved him, he would pack up and move on with his houseman, secretary and pilot. Everything he needed in his neat, orderly life. Anyone else would just be a hindrance.

Standing abruptly, Michelle said, "Maybe I'd better get busy on my papers. Do you think I should work in the library, Mac, or up in my room?"

"You may as well use the library, Mrs. Scott. Trang and I set up a table for you there. I think it's suitable for your work."

"All right, Mac," she said. Then, pausing, she added, "And, Mac. Please call me Michelle. Mrs. Scott seems too formal."

"Sure, Michelle," he said. "I'll be in the library in a little while. If you can't find what you need, holler."

"Thanks," she called, walking to the door.

In the library Michelle was relieved to see that Rick was not around. She hoped she could finish her paperwork before he came in. That way, she might be able to find some excuse to avoid seeing him any more than necessary. Trang and Mac seemed surprised by Rick's bad mood. She wasn't. He had seemed cold and unfriendly since she first arrived. Every day she had to stay here would probably just cause him to become even more distant.

She sighed and turned to her work. The sooner she got this over with, the sooner she could return to Detroit. And her dreary little apartment, and her job at Forest, if she still had a job after Rick took over the company. Gritting her teeth, she opened a notebook and began to write furiously.

As always, when Michelle set her mind on business, she managed to chase all other thoughts away. For the next several hours, she worked on the details of the merger.

When Mac entered the room and began to work at the small typing table, Michelle didn't feel distracted. She was accustomed to working with the sound of a typewriter clattering nearby. When she glanced up suddenly, however, and saw Rick's scowling face in the doorway, her heart lurched. She fastened her eyes on the page in front of her, hoping he hadn't noticed her glance at him. He continued to stand there for some time, until Mac suddenly looked up and saw him.

"Hi, boss. Are you looking for me?" Mac asked.

"No. Go ahead with your work, Mac," Rick replied. "I'm going upstairs to clean up."

Michelle looked over at Rick. He was dressed in a faded pair of coveralls, stained with grease. He turned swiftly on his heel and walked away.

Mac glanced over at Michelle and grinned. He stretched his arms above his head and sighed. "I've been typing so long, I'm stiff. Want to take a break?" he asked.

"Sounds like a good idea," she said.

As they walked toward the kitchen, Michelle asked, "Mac. Is there a bike around this place?"

He looked puzzled. "A bike? I haven't seen one. But I could try the basement. There's a pile of stuff stored down there. I guess Rick took possession of everything on the premises when he bought this place. I'll check it out later on." He glanced at her. "Need some exercise?"

"Yes. I get restless working all day at a desk. Besides," she added, "it would give me a chance to look over the town again."

As she put the kettle on for tea, Mac asked, "How long has it been since you were here, Michelle?"

Without turning around, she said softly, "Six years." She turned, and he noticed a wistful look on her face. "Sometimes it seems like six hundred years. Other times, it seems just like yesterday."

She shrugged and opened a cupboard. Mac watched for a moment as she stretched on tiptoe to reach the tea canister on the top shelf, then he crossed the kitchen to help her. As he reached up and handed it down to her, it slipped from her hands. Amid much noise and laughter, they both reached out and caught it in midair. They were both still laughing and holding tightly to the canister, when Michelle turned and caught sight of Rick standing in the doorway.

"Oh! Rick. You startled me!" she exclaimed.

Ignoring her, he asked Mac, "Where's Trang?"

"I don't know, Rick," he answered. "I haven't seen him. He's probably outside. Why?"

"I can't find the hand cleaner. The one I bought to remove oil," he said.

"I think Trang put it out in your workroom, so you wouldn't have to get oil and grease all over the doorknobs when you come in," Mac said. Then, glancing at the doorknob, he burst out laughing.

Rick's grim face slowly broke into a smile. "Uh huh. I'll bet you're right." Then, staring down at his grease-covered hands, he added, "So now, all the doorknobs in the house are covered with grease."

He headed out the back door, shaking his head.

Mac picked up the canister and looked questioningly at Michelle. "Why are you so quiet all of a sudden?" he asked.

"No reason," she said as she poured boiling water into the tea pot. The sight of Rick in the doorway had disturbed her. She was puzzled by the look on his face when he saw her laughing with Mac.

They sat at the kitchen table, quietly sipping their tea, when Trang walked in. Seeing them, he said, "Mac. I need some things in town. We go later on?"

"Sure, Trang. Let me know when you're ready." Then, turning to Michelle, he said as he winked his eye, "We can't let Trang take the car by himself. He'd rather run down everything in sight than turn the wheel. The only thing he knows how to work are the accelerator and the horn." Mac winked again, knowing Trang would rise to the bait.

"I am good driver," said Trang in agitation. "Mac knows I am good driver. He just wants excuse to go to town and look at the pretty girl in the restaurant."

Michelle laughed. "Ah, now I get it. So that's why you run so many errands for Rick. A waitress, huh?"

Mac grinned sheepishly. "You've got a big mouth, Trang," he said in mock anger.

A short while later, Mac and Trang left for town, still wrangling good-naturedly.

Alone in the house, Michelle prowled the library, picking up papers, then impatiently setting them back down. There seemed no use trying to get any more work done. Rick had left no notes or instructions, and she had no inclination to work alone.

Upstairs in her room, Michelle dressed in her old

jeans and sweater and dug out her canvas sneakers. She decided to search some of the outbuildings. Maybe there was still a bicycle on the premises, or a horse at a nearby stable—anything to get away for a while.

It was a brilliant autumn day. The sun had burned off all trace of frost from the leaf-covered lawn. The chill wind blowing off the lake left no doubt that winter was on its way.

Michelle walked briskly toward the stable, shading her eyes from the sun's reflection on the lake. She came around the building and pulled on the heavy wooden door.

Inside, Michelle stared around in surprise. Some of the stalls had been removed, others remained. Instead of harnesses and tack hanging about the walls, she saw tools of every size and shape. Track lighting had been installed along the ceiling, illuminating every corner of the huge room. All sorts of machines and engine parts were set about on waist-high pedestals. There was still a faint odor of manure, mixed with the much stronger odor of gasoline.

Michelle suddenly realized she wasn't alone. Rick was standing in the middle of the room, looking at her.

"Oh, I'm sorry, Rick. I didn't know anyone was in here. I thought I'd find a horse. But I can see there aren't any horses here anymore."

She stared at him, dressed in a mechanic's coverall. "What are you—oh, I see. This is a . . . your —workshop, isn't it?"

He wiped his hands on a rag and turned his back on her. "Yes. A workshop. I think of it as my lab. Where I try out my designs. I need a private place to work. This old stable suits me."

"And this is your latest design?" she asked, moving closer and pointing to the piece of machinery he had been working on.

"Yes." Rick moved back and regarded it as an artist might regard his latest work. "This is the prototype. If it works as well as I expect . . ." He shrugged and left the rest unsaid.

Michelle glanced at his rugged profile. His chin was lifted in defiance. His lips were pressed together firmly, his nostrils flaring. How much, she wondered, was riding on this prototype? His reputation? His integrity? His financial empire?

She turned suddenly. "Well, I'll get out of your way. I really didn't dream that anyone was in here. I'm sorry for interrupting," she said.

"Mike." He laid his hand on her arm, and she jumped nervously. He withdrew his hand, and held it stiffly by his side, clenching and unclenching his fist.

"Look," he said softly. "I'm sorry about last night."

She turned away from him. "It doesn't matter. . . ."

He grabbed her arm and forced her to turn back to him. "But it does matter." He was nearly shouting. "Mike! I feel rotten about what I said." He let go of her arm and raked his hand restlessly through his hair. Lowering his voice, he said, "The things I said last night were disgusting. I'd like you to accept my apology. And I'd like to start over." He stared intently at her.

Michelle couldn't meet his eyes. Instead, she stared, fascinated at the powerful muscles in his arm as he continued to clench and unclench his fist.

Moving out of his reach, she said, "Yes. Of course. We'll start over, Rick." Then she hurried from the building.

She had been unable to meet his eyes. How could she have allowed him to apologize! How could she go on with this lie, pretending a marriage that didn't exist, except in Rick's mind?

She hugged her arms about herself in the crisp air. *But,* another part of her mind argued, *this is the only defense I have against Rick. If he found out the truth, how vulnerable I really am to his charms, I'd be lost. What chance would I have alone with him, if he knew how I really felt? I have to keep a wedge between us.*

She hurried on toward the house. Still, despite her arguments with herself, the battle raged on in her mind. Rick's apology only added to her feelings of guilt. *Why is it, when I'm prepared for another battle of wits, he suddenly becomes gentle and . . . decent? And when I drop my guard, expecting tenderness, he reacts with anger and hostility?*

Michelle sighed as she entered the house. Worrying about Rick's attitude was definitely tiresome.

That evening, when Michelle came downstairs, she saw the dining room lights blazing. A round table had been set up near the French doors. Thankfully, she counted four places set for dinner. Obviously, Rick had reached the same conclusion as she—that they needed the company of Mac and Trang to fill the uncomfortable silences between them.

The cheerful banter between Mac and Trang enlivened the dinner hour. Michelle and Rick relaxed and found themselves chuckling at the gentle teasing and good humor of the two men.

After dinner, Mac said, "Trang and I are driving into town to see a movie. Why don't you two join us?"

Michelle glanced up in surprise. "Why, thanks Mac. I think that would be fun. I'll get my coat."

Mac turned to Rick. "How about you, boss?"

"No thanks, Mac. I have a lot of paper work to catch up on. I think I'll pass. But I appreciate the offer," he added.

The evening in town was a balm to Michelle's tightly strung nerves. There was much laughter and good-natured needling. Michelle's sunny humor responded to the silliness, and she found herself joining in the raucous laughter on the return drive.

They were still laughing uproariously as they walked into the silent Winter Castle late that night. As Michelle passed the library, she saw Rick still at work at his desk. His head shot up at the sound of her footsteps.

She called a hasty "Good night," and hurried up the stairs. It was late; she was deliciously relaxed and tired, and she had no desire to stick around and determine what kind of mood Rick might be in now.

Chapter Eight

In the days that followed, Michelle realized that Rick intended to stick to his offer to start over. They worked for several hours each day in the library. Usually, Mac's presence at the typewriter kept their conversations on an impersonal level.

In the afternoons, Rick worked alone in his lab. Often, he continued working through dinnertime and late into the night. Trang carried his meals to the converted stable, and fretted that his boss was not taking good care of himself.

On the evenings when he did join the others for dinner, Rick seemed withdrawn. Michelle feared that his experimental engine was not going as well as he had hoped.

Despite Trang's grumbling, Michelle discovered

that he had a real and deep affection for his boss. Mac, too, spoke highly of Rick.

"The boss works hard," Mac said. "And he plays fair too. No double dealing. No shortcuts. He's well respected in the business world. And," he added, "he plays hard too. We've taken some fantastic trips."

Trang nodded his agreement. "Mister Rick is a great guy," he affirmed.

Michelle smiled to herself. So much for her suspicions that Rick was a slave driver.

Finding herself alone in the kitchen one morning with Trang, Michelle casually asked him about his life in Vietnam.

Trang's eyes danced as he spoke lovingly about his home in Saigon. His features softened as he recalled his beloved home.

"French architecture," he said. "Very beautiful. We have a garden, inside a stone wall. My mother very proud of her garden. My father excellent cook. French and Vietnamese cuisine." He kissed his fingertips in a typically French gesture, and Michelle laughed.

"You and Henri LaRue should find you have a lot in common," she said.

Trang bristled. "Ha! That Frenchman who take over my kitchen?" He snorted. "What would we have in common?" he asked sarcastically.

"French cooking, for one thing," Michelle said. "Trang. I bet if you gave him a chance, you would find out that you would like Henri." She grinned at him. "And I'll bet you two would enjoy swapping recipes," she added.

"I think not, Missy," Trang said, frowning. "I boss of my kitchen."

As she sipped her coffee, Michelle asked, "Trang. How did you meet Rick?"

Trang clattered a pot in the sink, then turned off the water and faced her. A path of sunlight glistened on his coal-black hair. Michelle's eyes fell on his soft, almost delicate hands. A chef's hands. But those hands had been forced to hold a gun.

"I escape Vietnam in boat," he said. "There are eighty-four people aboard when we leave. By the time we arrive Philippines, there are fifty of us left. We are sent to a camp to wait for a place to go." Trang shrugged. "Any place all right with me. I am happy to be alive." Then he leaned forward in a conspiratorial fashion. "But Missy, in my heart, I long to go America. I had been friendly with American soldiers in Saigon. I dream of America. Freedom. Peace. A chance to work and live in a real house again." Trang wiped his hands on a towel and said sadly, "It was a long time since I live in a real house."

Then he brightened and said, "Mr. Rick visit the camp where I am sent in Philippines. He is friend of American doctor at camp." With a smile, he added, "Americans are easy to spot. They taller than anyone else around. Stand out in crowd." Then he went on. "All kinds of people rush over whenever an American visits the camp. Women, children, all hoping they can get permission to leave. I think to myself, 'If I can just get chance to talk to that tall American, I will convince him to take me with him.' But so many people around him." Trang shook his head slowly as he recalled the past. "I see him clap his hands on the doctor's shoulders, then shake his hand. I know the tall American is getting ready to leave the camp. How can I get close to him? He is starting to walk away. The crowd around him grows thicker. Babies crying. Women shouting. Children shrieking. How can I make the tall American notice me?"

Michelle was staring intently at Trang. She sat on the edge of her chair.

Trang continued. "The American moves slowly toward the gate. He calls out, and the gate is opening. I begin to shout. Nobody can hear me. He is walking through the gate, toward a car parked nearby. The gate is swinging shut behind him. Still the crowds are too thick to get close to him."

Michelle interrupted, "Oh, Trang. What did you do?"

Trang's eyes were wide. "I know this my last chance to get the American's attention. I am desperate. I remember what an American soldier teach me in Saigon. I put my fingers to my lips and whistle—so loud—like this."

Trang put his fingers to his lips and whistled shrilly.

Michelle stared at him in amazement. "Trang! That's beautiful! I thought I was the only one who could whistle like that," she said, suddenly laughing.

Trang beamed proudly. "You know what Mr. Rick do when I whistle?" he asked.

Michelle shook her head.

"Mr. Rick turn and stare at the crowd. So I put my fingers up to my mouth and whistle again. Mr. Rick walk back through the gate and stare at me.

"He say to me, 'Who teach you to whistle like that?'"

Trang was clearly enjoying his story now. He flashed a wide grin at Michelle.

"I say to Mr. Rick, 'American soldier teach me.'

"And Mr. Rick starts to laugh. And I say to him, 'I had to get you to notice me. It the only thing I can think of. I am good cook. Take me to America and I fatten you up.' And Mr. Rick laugh again. He shake his head from side to side and say, 'What your name?' And I tell him, 'Trang.' And he say to me, 'Trang. I only know one other person in whole world who can whistle like that. And if I can't have her cook for me, I might as well have you.'"

Michelle felt a lump rising to her throat. Finding it difficult to speak, Michelle swallowed, then asked, "Did you experience any culture shock when you arrived in America?"

Trang stared at her for a long moment of silence. His face, normally so filled with emotion, became bland, expressionless. Then, very quietly, he said, "Any country which survives war, Missy, is in constant state of shock. To witness birth, when all around you dying. To see food wasted, when many starve. Missy, I am, . . ." he groped for the correct word, "beyond shock."

There was a long silence while Trang clattered pots and pans in the sink. Michelle sipped her coffee, lost in thought.

When Trang turned around again, his smile was dazzling. "And now you know how I come to America. I just whistle and I have a home."

Trang put his hands on his hips and stared at Michelle. "You like my story, Missy?"

Michelle was smiling tenderly at Trang, but there were misty tears welling up in her emerald eyes. "Yes, Trang. I liked your story very much," she said softly. Then she ducked her head and sipped her coffee, while Trang went about his morning chores. He had told her much more than he knew.

One afternoon the sunlight beckoned her outdoors. Stepping through the French doors, she stood on the brick-paved courtyard and surveyed the brilliant autumn foliage. Here, in sloping banks and along the walkways grew mums in every imaginable size and color. Huge clay pots spilled over with mums that had grown rangy and ragged from neglect.

Michelle knelt down and lifted a heavy pot lying on its side. Although it was cracked and leaking soil, the tenacious plants still grew. Spotting a rusted hand trowel half-buried in the earth, Michelle pulled it toward her and began shoveling in dirt around the roots of the plants. Moving slowly along on her knees, she began rearranging the pots in some kind of order, throwing bits of broken pottery in a pile near the door, cutting away some of the more ragged plants and digging up buried bricks that had once formed a neat border.

This was a pleasant break from the routine of paper work. Without realizing it, Michelle wiped her brow, leaving a trail of dirt across her forehead. She leaned back on her heels and surveyed her work. The flower bed nearest the door was now neatly turned and pruned, contrasting sharply with the overgrown beds all around. Michelle sighed contentedly.

Even though the air was sharp and cold, the sun had managed to warm her through her clothing. She rolled back the cuffs of her long-sleeved shirt and glanced at the dirty smudges in dismay. Without garden gloves her fingernails were caked with mud, and her hands were black. She shrugged in indifference. It didn't matter. It felt good just to be outside, making some order of the disarray.

Lifting another broken pot, she began fitting the larger pieces together like a jigsaw puzzle. She was humming to herself, thinking that she might be able to mend this pot with a little glue.

When Rick's voice sounded directly behind her, she jumped in alarm.

"Playing house?" he asked sarcastically.

"Oh!" Michelle dropped the pieces of crockery and turned to stare up at him. "I didn't hear you coming. Now look what you made me do," she moaned.

He glanced down at the broken pot, then at her stricken face. "Leave it Mike. It's just an old clay pot," he said.

She picked up the pieces and dropped them in the pile of broken pottery by the door. Rick moved closer to her. With his finger, he traced the dirty smudges she had left across her forehead.

"Were you having a good time, Mike?" he asked gently.

Michelle made a face. "Yes. It was fun," she admitted. "But I'm sorry about the time. I didn't realize how long I've been out here. I didn't mean to let my work go, Rick. Have you been waiting for me?"

"The paper work doesn't matter," he said.

He glanced down at the flower bed. "It looks good, Mike. I didn't know you liked to work outside."

She shrugged. "I've never had much time for it. But when I was a little girl, we had a Japanese gardener. I used to follow him around, pestering him with a million questions. He never seemed to mind, though. In fact, one summer, he taught me a little about Bonsai. You know. Miniature trees and plants . . ."

They were standing so close together, they were touching. Michelle suddenly felt very self-conscious. She stared down at her dirt-smeared hands. As she moved to put them behind her back, Rick caught her hands in his and stared down at them. She marveled at the power in his grip. Strong, yet tender. As she started to pull her hands away, he held them tighter. She glanced up at him through her long lashes, feeling her cheeks burn at his gaze.

Very firmly he placed her hands around his waist.

Then he gently slid his hands up around her shoulders.

"I'll get your shirt all dirty," she protested.

"Uh humm," he murmured against her ear.

"Rick. My hands are filthy. I'll ruin your shirt," she said, pushing against him.

"Good," he said, nuzzling her cheek. "I can't think of a nicer way to get dirty." He kissed the tip of her nose. "Besides, your face is all dirty, so my shirt might as well be dirty too," he said.

"What!" She pulled back. "Where is my face dirty?"

He pulled her roughly into his arms. Kissing her forehead, he murmured, "Here. And here. And over here."

At the touch of his lips, a delicious tingle began low in her spine. She stopped struggling and stood very still. Sensing her reaction, Rick paused for a moment, then bent and kissed her lips. As her lips parted and she returned his kiss, the flame spread through her body, reaching even her fingertips. Michelle felt as though she were on fire.

Burying his face in her hair, Rick murmured, "I should know better, Mike. But I can't help it. I know that holding you like this—kissing you—is only going to make things worse. But, oh, Mike!" and he brought his lips to her waiting mouth.

She clung to him weakly. It was an exquisite pain, holding him, wanting him. Then, all too soon, Rick stiffened slightly and moved back.

Michelle heard footsteps coming across the dining room. Rick stepped back another pace.

"Tell Mac I've decided to work in my lab for a while," he said gruffly.

Then he turned and she was left to face Mac alone.

For days Rick had been locking himself away in his workroom in the stable. Michelle was eager to know how his work was progressing, but whenever she asked Mac or Trang, they admitted that they knew as little as she about Rick's work.

Several times, while she and Rick were working in the library, she asked him about his prototype. He was always vague, saying only that the work was progressing satisfactorily.

Late one afternoon, while Mac and Trang were in town, Rick came rushing in the back door, wiping his hands on a towel. He started past the library, when he caught sight of Michelle working at her desk.

He stood framed in the doorway. There was a sense of urgency about the way he stood tensely, holding his unleashed energy in check.

"Mike. How would you like to go for a ride?" he asked quietly.

"Mac has the car, Rick. He drove Trang into town for some things," she replied.

"I have another car," he said. "I keep it in a shed in the back."

She stared at him in surprise. Then, deciding quickly, she said, "Just wait until I get my jacket upstairs."

"I'll wait for you in the driveway," he called.

Michelle flew upstairs, glancing in the mirror for a quick glimpse of her hair and makeup, and grabbed her jacket from the closet.

A low, sleek, silver car Michelle had never seen before sat idling in the driveway. Rick sat behind the wheel. He had removed his work overalls, revealing dark brown corduroy slacks and a beige flannel shirt, the sleeves rolled up above his elbows.

Michelle slid in the passenger side and closed the door. She stared around the plush interior admiringly.

"Rick. This is beautiful. What's it called?" she asked.

"I haven't given it a name yet," he said. "It's still in the experimental stage."

He leaned across the seat to help her into a safety harness. He pulled the strap firmly across her stomach, and snapped it shut.

"To get out of all this gear in a hurry, Mike, just press this gadget," he said, indicating a round, flat disc.

Michelle pressed where he pointed, and with a slight click the harness and safety belt fell away and disappeared beneath the seat.

"Good," he said with a slow smile of satisfaction. "Now pull here."

Michelle did as he said, and the harness and belt reappeared.

Rick once again helped her into the safety gear, bending forward to check a strap. As he leaned across her, she could smell the faint soap scent and the stronger odor of gasoline, which still clung to his clothes. She longed to reach out and touch the dark silky hair which dipped across his forehead as he moved. As he snapped the belt shut, his hand brushed across her breast. She felt him stiffen slightly, then move away.

"All set?" he asked as he adjusted his own safety gear.

She nodded stiffly.

Rick glanced across at her. "All this is a little confining," he said. "but it isn't uncomfortable," he added, as if reading her mind. "Even though this is an experimental car, it's been tested thoroughly. I wouldn't take you along if there were any danger," he assured her. "But I have to take these precautions."

Michelle smiled at him. "I'm not worried, Rick. I know you wouldn't take any chances. I trust you."

He held her gaze a moment longer. "I hope you don't mind if we don't talk for a while, Mike. I want to listen to this engine," he said.

"I won't say a word until you say it's all right," she promised.

Rick put the car in gear and started out the driveway. Michelle leaned back and watched his hands on the wheel of the car. Dark hairs gleamed along the exposed forearms. He expertly maneuvered the car along the twisting, rutted road leading to the highway. Once on the highway leading to town, the car moved along smoothly. As they came to the top of a hill, Michelle drank in the beauty of the scenery before her. To her right lay the lake, glistening like diamonds in the brilliant sunshine. To the left lay a pastoral scene more perfect than any artist's canvas. Gently rolling brown hills, stripped of their crop of hay, ended in a wooded area thick with fiery autumn foliage—dark red sumac, with their velvety purple spikes, bright yellow elm and poplar, and red and orange oak leaves.

Rick stopped the car and pointed to a stand of trees.

"Look, Mike."

She followed the direction he was pointing out and caught her breath. A deer stood, unmoving, its head lifted as if to catch their scent. It paused a moment longer, then darted to the safety of the woods.

Rick shifted gears and they drove off more slowly. Michelle strained to catch sight of more deer in the woods and barren field, but she saw none.

They drove through town and beyond, along a nearly deserted stretch of highway. Finally satisfied, Rick turned back and headed toward town.

Michelle was grateful that she hadn't had to make conversation. It was pleasant just riding, allowing her thoughts to drift. It had been a companionable silence.

When Rick turned down a familiar street, Michelle stiffened. "Why are we turning here, Rick?" she asked.

"I thought you might like to see how The Oaks looks after all these years," he remarked.

"The Oaks," she repeated softly.

"Would you like to see it?" he asked.

"Yes. I think I would," she answered.

They drove slowly. Michelle's throat felt dry. As

they pulled up in front of the drive, Michelle stared at the old, familiar house. The wide porch which ran the length of the house had been freshly painted, as well as the fence in front. A new, darker roof had been added. The grounds were perfectly manicured. Rick turned off the engine and walked around to Michelle's side of the car. She fumbled with the disc which released the safety harness. Rick held her door, and she stepped out of the car. Rick followed her up the driveway.

No one seemed to be around. The house had been carefully closed up for its long winter rest. They followed the driveway to the rear of the house. Walking up the back steps, Michelle crossed the porch and peered in the small windowpane of the back door. A kitchen table and several chairs were all that she could see.

She turned and walked to the garage. Standing on tiptoe, Michelle could make out a child's red wagon loaded with several sand buckets for the beach. She smiled to herself. So the people who bought her house had children. That pleased her. She wondered who slept in her old bedroom now. She hoped it was a little girl. One who would appreciate the special vanity her father had designed for her. It had a small, hidden drawer for special treasures. She was smiling as she turned from the garage.

She glanced on the porch for Rick. He wasn't there. She turned. Rick was standing at the rose arbor, one hand thrust in his pocket, the other hand leaning against the arch. He watched her as she walked toward him.

"Are you glad you came?" he asked.

"Yes. Whoever bought the place must care about it. It's in great shape," she said. "And they have children. I saw a wagon and some sand buckets in the garage. Isn't that great?"

Rick smiled indulgently. "Yes. That's great," he said, then he reached out and gently pulled her into the circle of his arms.

"No, Rick," she said, resisting. "Not here."

"Oh yes, Mike," he growled. "Especially here. The scene of the crime. Remember?" He began kissing her lips, slowly nibbling away her resistance.

Did she remember? As his lips began devouring hers, all the passion she had felt that night washed over her. Her hands spread across his rib cage, then slid around his waist. His kiss was like a powerful drug, weakening her against her will. Rick nibbled her ear lobe, then burned a trail of fiery kisses down her neck. When he bent his lips to the base of her throat, her hands reached up to his shoulders, the fingernails biting into his flesh as she tried to hold on.

Michelle had no will left. This perfect afternoon, this old familiar beloved house and this man in her arms had all conspired to defeat her resolve. She had no pride left. She wanted Rick, and she hoped he felt the same way about her.

Rick raised his head. His smoldering gaze lingered on her mouth. He ran his finger lightly over her lips. A breeze lifted a strand of her hair, blowing it across her eyes. He reached up and smoothed it, then caught at her thick hair and watched as the silken strands slipped from his fingers.

"I remember that golden summer, Mike," he said softly. "I wish we could have stopped time."

"I know," she said, her throat aching from unshed tears. "But it's too late, Rick."

He traced the collar of her shirt with his finger, dipping down where it was unbuttoned, stopping short when his finger touched the silky fabric of her bra. She stood very still, watching his eyes. They narrowed suddenly, and he reached down and caught her hand in his.

"Come on, Mike. This always leads up to a fight," he said, suddenly gruff. He pulled her roughly back to the car.

As they adjusted their safety gear in silence, Rick looked over suddenly at Michelle, "Are you sorry you came back to see The Oaks?" he asked sharply.

Her voice caught in her throat. "Oh no, Rick. I think I would have been—not afraid—but reluctant to come back here alone. But now that I've seen it, I feel better. The people who bought it must love it as much as my family did."

As they drove away, Michelle turned and watched until the house was out of sight.

On the drive back, Rick and Michelle were silent, each lost in private thoughts.

Michelle closed her eyes. She could recall every detail of The Oaks as it had looked when she had lived there. The grandfather clock in the hallway. The frilly white bedspread in her room. The windowseat, covered in her grandmother's petit pointe roses. On hot summer nights, she would curl up in the cushions there and daydream about her future. She could recall the heady scent of the rose arbor.

Every little detail about that night with Rick was etched vividly in her mind. Her cheeks burned suddenly. She opened her eyes and stole a quick glance at Rick's strong profile.

How did he remember that night? Did it amuse him to think of her clumsy attempts to seduce him?

"Rick McCord can have any girl he wants, Baby Sister." Connie's hateful words rang in her brain. And he hadn't wanted her.

She turned her head swiftly and stared out the window. She could no longer bear to look at the proud, arrogant man seated next to her.

When they arrived back at the Winter Castle, Rick drove around to the back of the house. In front of a weatherbeaten shed, he pressed a button on the dashboard, and the door lifted up, revealing the inside. Rick drove in and turned off the ignition. He pressed the button again, and the door dropped down silently. Lights went on automatically, illuminating another workroom. This one was smaller than the room Rick used to work on his prototype. This appeared to be just a garage, with a long work table along one wall. Various tools hung on orderly racks above the workbench. A rack had been installed on the floor to raise and lower the car. A winch hung overhead to facilitate installing the engines in the car.

Michelle released her safety harness and opened

the door. Rick got out and lifted the hood of the car. He seemed unaware of her presence.

As he bent under the hood, Michelle asked, "Are you pleased with the engine?"

"Not completely," he said. He reached to the workbench and picked up a notebook. Flipping pages, he began to write furiously. When Michelle glanced back at him before leaving the shed, he was still making notations in his book.

"Thanks for the ride, Rick. I'll leave you to your work," she called.

He was so distracted, he didn't even respond. He had closed her out of his life—perhaps for good. She closed the door softly and walked to the house.

Chapter Nine

It was a Friday night. Michelle was especially happy and excited because Burt Matheson was flying in on Saturday, and she had given him a list of things she wanted. She was sick of the same old clothes every day. It would be a relief to wear a few different things. And she needed warmer clothes. The nights had grown increasingly colder.

Mac and Trang drove into town to see a new movie. Michelle went up to her room to read. Rick had been locked alone in his workroom for hours.

Michelle set aside her book. She was restless. She paced the floor, then grabbed her sweater and walked downstairs. A glance out the French doors revealed a hazy sun setting across the lake. She pushed open the doors and strolled toward the water's edge.

Wisps of fog hung just above the water. More fog drifted across the sloping lawn. Michelle climbed atop a huge rock jutting into the water, and hugged her arms about her drawn-up knees.

She watched the lone flight of a gull, dipping into the waves, then soaring skyward with its catch. It was so peaceful here. How could she bear to leave this place behind when her work was completed here? How could she go back to the city traffic, the cramped apartment, the endless noise intruding on her every waking moment?

Michelle thought about Rick, and how his very presence dwarfed all other men she had ever met. If she could be eighteen again, and all that had happened in the past six years could be erased . . . She smiled dreamily.

She shivered and glanced toward the stable. She was startled. There was no trace of the building. She couldn't even see the lights of the house. A thick blanket of fog had covered every trace of life.

She scrambled down from the rock. Water lapped at her feet, soaking her canvas shoes and socks, and the cuffs of her jeans. She scurried out of the water's reach and stopped in her tracks. Which way was back?

She walked a short way, then suddenly a tree loomed up in front of her. She let out a gasp. There was no big tree between the house and the lake. She must have veered to the side. She stopped and stared around her. There was nothing but the damp, thick fog.

Michelle clenched her fists in anger and frustration. How could she have been so careless? She had seen the first signs of the fog rolling in and had foolishly ignored them.

During her youthful summers here she had heard many frightening stories about the treacherous fog. The Coast Guard had often had to rescue inexperienced yachtsmen who naively thought they could reach a safe harbor in the fog. Many fishermen were forced to spend entire nights in their small boats after becoming lost in thick fog. Everyone in this area was familiar with the horrible stories of larger craft colliding with smaller boats in dense fogbanks.

Michelle stood still and fought to overcome the strangling panic which caught in her throat. Mac and Trang were surely trapped in town by this fog. They would never be able to maneuver the narrow, twisting roads tonight. That left only Rick. But he often worked in his lab until late into the night. If he had become caught up in an experiment, he wouldn't even be aware of the weather outside. And he had no idea that she wasn't safely relaxing back in the house.

Her wet feet were becoming numb with cold. She was trembling violently. She fought to remain calm. The house was only a few hundred yards from the lake. But if she got turned in the wrong direction, she could walk all night, skirting the lake and traveling through acres of deserted property.

She must find a landmark. The willows! She turned back and made her way slowly. Finally, the frigid waters of the lake washed over her ankles. She should have reached the willows before she came in contact with the waters of the lake. This meant that she was far to the left or right of the point she wanted to reach.

Stay calm! she told herself. *If I follow the shore, I have to come to the willows.*

She walked for perhaps fifteen minutes, forcing herself to stay at the water's edge. After a while, she even stopped jumping back when a wave washed over her feet. She turned and made her way back along the edge of the lake, knowing that she would have to eventually find the willows.

There was no feeling left in her feet. She had never been so cold in her life. Suddenly, in the thick vapor which kept her from seeing anything, wispy tendrils of willow branches brushed across her head and face. She cried out in terror, then sank to her knees in relief. She had reached the willows! Now, if she could walk a straight line to the house, she would reach safety.

Turning away from the lake, Michelle began the slow ascent from the shore toward the house. But, without realizing it, she was moving at an angle toward Rick's workroom.

Michelle nearly bumped into the stable before she realized it was in front of her. With a cry of relief, she pushed her weight against the door. It was locked. She pounded her fists on the door in frustration.

"Rick! Rick! Open up! Please hurry! Rick!"

There was no sound from within. Michelle sunk down on her knees before the bolted door. He had gone back to the house. Perhaps to bed. He wouldn't even know she was missing until morning. She pressed her forehead against the door, sobbing bitterly.

A distant sound caused Michelle to jerk her head up. She strained to hear something more. A moment later, she heard it again. A call! She stood and cupped her hands to her mouth.

She stayed at the door of the stable, afraid that if she left this landmark, she would again be lost in the dense fog. Again and again she shouted, then listened for an answering call. She shouted until she was hoarse. Still the calls seemed to be no closer.

Frustrated, she choked back tears of anger. As a last resort, Michelle put her two fingers to her mouth and whistled shrilly. A few moments later, an answering call sounded closer. She continued the shrill whistle. Suddenly, a tiny pinpoint of light gleamed through the dense fog. Michelle whistled as loudly as she could.

Strong arms gripped her trembling shoulders.

"Mike! Oh, thank God!"

Rick enfolded her in his arms, and she leaned against him weakly.

"Can you walk, Mike?" he asked.

"Yes. I think so. If you lead, I'll follow. My feet are so numb, they don't even hurt anymore," she moaned.

She was lifted and carried in powerful strides toward the house.

As she wrapped her arms tightly around Rick's neck, she heard his deep, warm chuckle. "Thank goodness you're a little tomboy who learned how to whistle. Otherwise, I don't think I would have ever found you. Do you know how long I've been calling you?" he asked.

"No," she said against his warm cheek.

"It seems like hours," he whispered tenderly. I'll never forget the first time I ever heard you do that, Mike. When you called back your horse, remember?"

She burrowed her cold face down into the warmth of his neck and murmured, "I was whistling for my trusty steed. And this time my knight in shining armor showed up to rescue me."

"No knight," he said softly. "Just a mere man, Mike."

Rick carried her to the sofa in the library. As she lay back against the cushions, he pulled off her soaked shoes and socks.

"Get those wet clothes off," he ordered. "I'll find a blanket."

Within minutes, he returned with a woolen blanket. Michelle had struggled out of her jeans and sweater. Rick knelt and built up a fire while Michelle removed her soaked underclothes and snuggled into the scratchy warmth of the blanket.

Rick walked to the bar and poured brandy into two glasses. Handing one to her, he gulped the other and stared down at her.

"How did you know I was out there?" she asked.

"When I found the house empty, I assumed you had gone to town with Mac and Trang."

"That's what I was afraid of," she whispered.

"Then Mac phoned to say he and Trang would have to spend the night in town at the Harbor House. The fog was too thick to try the roads back."

Rick ran his hand through his damp hair. "As Mac was hanging up, he said, 'Tell Michelle I didn't make up this fog story just so I could spend more time with my waitress.'"

Rick shook his head as he added, "I was floored! I said to Mac, 'You mean Mike isn't with you?' When he said you were here, I was puzzled."

Rick knelt down and took her hands in both of his. "Mike, I searched every room in this house. Then I realized you were out there somewhere in the fog."

Michelle shivered. "It was such a stupid thing to do. I noticed the fog rolling in, but I just didn't pay any attention to it. I was down near the lake, just sorting out my thoughts." She stared into his eyes. "Rick, I tried not to panic. I thought if I stayed calm, I could make my way back to the house. But when I reached your lab and found it locked, I really fell apart. If I hadn't heard you shouting and realized you were aware I was out there, I think I would have given up."

Rick sat down and wrapped his arms around her. "Not you, Mike. You're not one to quit. You're a survivor. We both know that."

He cupped his hands on either side of her face and stared into her eyes. The flame of his passion burned her skin.

He pulled her closer and murmured against her temple. "When I realized you were lost out there in that fog, I nearly went crazy. I figured I'd lost you again."

He felt her tremble, and pulled her gently against him. "You're safe now, Mike," he murmured against her hair.

"Am I?" she whispered.

He glanced down into her eyes. "What do you mean?" He added softly, "I'll hold you and keep you safe."

He bent and nuzzled her neck, and she felt the heat begin to spread through her body.

Michelle slid her hands from beneath the folds of the blanket and tentatively touched the stubble of beard on his chin. He moved his face against her hand. Then, his mouth descended to her lips and he began a gentle probing kiss. Michelle twined her arms around his neck and returned his kiss without restraint.

The rough blanket slipped down and Rick brought his lips to the exposed skin of her shoulder. Flames ignited between them, and they came together in a kiss so passionate they seemed fused together.

As Rick's hands slipped inside the blanket to draw her even closer, she reacted with shock when his hands touched her bare skin.

As much as she wanted him, she knew it couldn't be like this. She had wanted his love, for a lifetime. Not for an evening. Not to be discarded in the morning, in the light of day.

Suddenly, she turned from him. "No, Rick! Please," she whispered.

Rick caressed her arm with his fingertips and bent

to kiss the back of her neck. As she shivered, he rained feather-light kisses from one naked shoulder to the other. Michelle felt her resolve slipping.

In a gentle, coaxing voice he whispered, "Mike. Turn around and look at me. Tell me with your eyes that you don't want me."

She shivered and clutched her hands to her breast, to hold what little blanket she could to cover her. Rick continued kissing the back of her neck, brushing aside her silken hair with his hand.

The fire, the brandy and Rick's gentle touch had a hypnotic effect on Michelle. She thought how good it would be to lie in his arms, to finally end this terrible tension between them.

Trembling, she turned and stared into his eyes. He could see the desire in them.

"Oh, Mike. I've wanted you for such a long time!" he breathed.

She closed her eyes as his mouth covered hers tenderly. He wanted her. But it would never be enough. Because she wanted his love. And Rick McCord, she thought, takes what he wants. He doesn't love.

She twisted free of his arms. "No, Rick. Don't!" she said, struggling to keep the tremor from her voice.

"What!" he exclaimed. "Why, Mike?" he asked, suddenly angry.

"I've been afraid of something like this," she said. "Working together, being thrown together constantly. It isn't love that's driving us to this, Rick. It's just . . . I don't know. Maybe remembering. Maybe just that we've spent too much time together. I just know I can't, Rick. Not like this," she added.

His puzzled look turned to an angry frown.

"Why not, Mike? When you were that innocent little eighteen-year-old, you offered yourself to me. You were mine for the taking. And, like a fool, I chose the honorable way. I didn't want to spoil what we had. So we ended up having nothing. And you couldn't wait to give your love to someone— anyone —willing. Is that why you couldn't wait for me, Mike? Is it because I had awakened a desire in you, and when I left, you looked around for someone else? How long did it take you to find your new love?"

Michelle buried her face in her hands to stop his cruel words.

A muscle worked tensely in his jaw. "Mike. I can't go on like this. You're driving me crazy! Living in this house, sleeping in the next room. Sometimes, late at night, I get out of bed and pace the floor. How easy it would be to just force my way into your room. You'll never know how many nights I've stood outside your door, waging a battle with myself."

His lips sought hers. A searing fire blazed within her. She wanted him more than she had ever wanted anything in her life. But she recalled that summer years ago. If he had made love to her that night in the rose arbor, she would have had to carry the additional burden of guilt along with her father's scandal. Because she knew that making love that night wouldn't have changed anything. Her father would have still found out about her and Rick from

Connie. He would have still gone to Rick's family. And Rick's father would have still accused her father of fraud and theft. And, worst of all, Rick would have still gone away, leaving her not only alone and bereft, but soiled by it all as well.

Abruptly, she stood, clutching the blanket about her. Through gritted teeth, she hissed, "No Rick! I can't. Don't touch me! Please. Just leave me alone!"

Rick's passion turned to anger. He stared at her in disbelief. Michelle closed her eyes to blot out his fury. How much more painful it would be if she tasted the exquisite joy of his lovemaking, and then had to be denied it for the rest of her life. This would be better, in time. She would make a clean break. She clenched her fists. She would survive. She had survived worse.

She heard Rick's voice, choked with rage. "You've never really forgotten, or forgiven, have you, Mike?" Then he said in a tightly controlled monotone, "I wonder if your husband appreciates his wife's fidelity."

Scalding tears forced themselves from between her closed lids. Angrily, she brushed them away with the back of her hand.

A moment later, the door of the library slammed with a force which sent sparks flying in the fireplace.

Then there was only the sound of Rick's footsteps echoing along the halls as he climbed the stairs to his room.

Chapter Ten

Rain pelted the kitchen windows. Michelle sat alone at the table, gratefully sipping a cup of strong coffee.

She had stayed up in her room all morning, hoping to avoid seeing Rick. She took a shower, washed her hair, blew it dry, rummaged around the room, deliberately wasting time. Finally, just when she thought she could stand it no longer, she had heard the front door slam, and a few minutes later, the roar of a car engine.

Michelle had crept stealthily down the stairs, still afraid she might meet Rick. She was relieved when a careful search of the downstairs rooms revealed she was alone.

The shrill ringing of the telephone startled her.

"Michelle?" It was Mac's voice. "Trang and I are in Petoskey. Do you need anything?"

"Petoskey!" She paused. "What are you doing there?"

"The boss called the Harbor House early this morning and told us to drive over here to pick up some auto engine parts." He waited a moment, then asked, "Hey, Michelle. What happened to him last night?"

Michelle nervously tucked her hair behind her ear and switched the phone to the other side. "What do you mean by that, Mac?"

"Something must have really set him off, Michelle. I've never heard the boss in such a foul mood."

"I—I can't imagine, Mac," she hedged. "I just came downstairs a few minutes ago. Rick is gone."

"Yeah. He said he was driving the experimental car out to the airport to meet his lawyer, Burt Matheson. If you're smart, Michelle, you'll keep out of his way until he works out whatever is bothering him," Mac advised.

"Yes. Thanks, Mac. Good advice. Well, I really don't need anything from the store. I'll see you later."

Michelle picked up her coffee cup and walked to the windows. The rain was splattering thickly against the windowpane, then running down in little rivulets. The temperature had been dropping all morning. Already the rain was turning to sleet. By night time it would probably be snowing. The dreary weather matched her mood perfectly.

She refilled her coffee cup and walked down the

hallway to the library. No cheery fire greeted her. She set down her cup and stirred the ashes with a poker. The dead ashes of last night's fire, she thought sadly. She didn't really think a fire would improve anything, but she needed to be busy.

Picking up several logs, she tossed them in the fireplace and added some kindling. A short time later, the fire was crackling.

Michelle moved to the window and stared through the rain and sleet to the lake beyond. In the light of day, it appeared to be just a strenuous walk along weed-choked paths and walkways. But in the thick fog of last night, the distance from lake to house had become a nightmare.

She stared at the willows down by the water's edge, their branches flailing in the wind that was whipping across the water. Then her glance moved to Rick's workshop in the stable. The distances didn't seem so great in the light of day.

Michelle sighed and walked to her desk. She had come to a decision during the long hours of the night, as she lay awake, agonizing over her relationship with Rick. When they had a chance to talk, she would insist that he make arrangements for her return to Detroit. Neither of them could go on working effectively under this strain.

She knew if she stayed here any longer, Rick would gain control of her emotions and wear down her resistance.

Last night had been the final straw. Michelle wanted Rick so badly, that she still felt an empty ache deep inside. And if she gave in to Rick's persuasions, how long could she hope to keep him here with her?

Hadn't Mac and Trang said that Rick often grew restless, packing up and leaving at will? Michelle looked around the unkempt room. This was just a temporary place for Rick to work on his latest project. He showed no interest in making this a permanent home. She shivered. If she let herself love him, when he finally grew restless and left her, the void in her life would be unbearable.

She stood suddenly and walked to Rick's desk. Picking up some papers, she decided to force herself to concentrate on her work. It was certainly better than dwelling on her personal problems.

She only half-heard the crunch of the tires in the driveway, the slam of the front door. It was when Rick strode through the doorway of the library and stood scowling at her that Michelle looked up in surprise.

"Mike! Go and pack. I've instructed my pilot to hold the plane for you." His sharp, staccato words struck her with the impact of bullets.

"What? I don't understand, Rick," she said, stunned.

"Don't you? I'm giving you what you wanted from the beginning. Your freedom. You're free to go, Mike."

She stared at the imposing figure filling the room with his electric energy.

It was the only solution, of course. She had arrived at the same decision during the agonizing hours of the night. But the fierceness of Rick's anger shocked her.

"You're right, of course," she said slowly. "I had decided to talk to you about it later anyway. But with this weather so severe, I'm a little afraid to fly today, Rick. Would you mind if I waited a day or so until the weather cleared?"

"Yes. I would mind," he snapped. "I want you out of this house today!"

From the beginning of their working relationship, Michelle had always been conscious of her quick temper. She had carefully schooled herself to keep it in check. Now, stung by his arrogant attitude, something in Michelle snapped.

Hands on her hips, she shouted, "I'm telling you, Rick. I won't fly in this weather. Order your precious pilot to come back for me tomorrow. Look out that window. The temperature has dropped. The rain is freezing. If you want me dead, you'll have to find another way. I'm not flying in this."

She flung him a hate-filled look, then dropped her eyes as he fixed her with a cold stare. He took a step closer to her, and his voice dropped to nearly a whisper.

"During the course of my conversation with Burt Matheson this morning, I asked him about your husband."

Michelle flinched.

"Burt told me your husband is dead. He said the marriage was really only a legal technicality anyway, whatever than means."

Rick's face was dark with rage. He ran his hand distractedly through his hair. "I asked Burt how the hell he could say that. He told me it was none of my business. He told me that he had already said too much. He said that if you had wanted me to know, you would have told me yourself."

Michelle's mouth dropped open in surprise. She couldn't speak.

Rick took a step closer, holding his clenched fists rigidly by his side. The controlled fury within him frightened her.

"I could gratefully strangle you with my bare hands, Mike!"

Then, suddenly, he turned his back on her shocked expression and headed toward the door. He said in clipped, precise tones, "It doesn't matter now. Nothing matters anymore. When you didn't even have the decency to answer my letters, I knew you couldn't find it in your heart to forgive me for what my father did. I have no right to question the things you did to survive."

Michelle was so hurt and angry that she barely heard what Rick was saying. All that she had taken in was the cold tone that told her that he wanted her out of the house.

"I'm leaving! I'm leaving!" she screamed. She wanted to shout the house down, but she tried to control herself as she said bitingly between clenched teeth, "I know it would please you if I could leave immediately. But, I'm sorry, Rick, I won't fly in this weather. Tell your pilot to be ready to fly me out of here the minute the weather clears. And not a minute sooner! I value my life, even if you don't!"

"OK, Mike," he said indifferently. "In the meantime, go up and pack your things. I don't want you around a minute longer than necessary. Just get out of my life, Mike."

Rick turned and strode from the room. A moment later, the front door slammed. A car engine sounded. Tires squealed. And she was alone.

Michelle stood unmoving before the fireplace. Long after the fire had burned down to a pile of burning embers, she stood frozen to the spot.

She turned suddenly, as if from a trance. She had no idea how long she had been there, too shocked to think or to focus on what to do next.

Now, she realized the enormity of the scene she had enacted with Rick. It was over. She must go upstairs and pack.

In the upstairs hallway, as Michelle passed the master bedroom where Rick slept, she stopped and retraced her steps to the door. It was standing slightly open. Though she knew she had no right, Michelle couldn't resist the temptation to look inside.

Pausing just inside the doorway, she glanced

around at the polished wood paneling and tipped her head back to stare at the high, beamed ceiling.

The focal point of the room was a massive, fourposter bed set on a raised section of the floor. Luxurious carpeting, thick enough to sink into, covered the floor and the steps leading to the bed.

Furtively, she crossed the room to stare into the huge, walk-in closet. Rick's clothes hung in orderly rows along the walls. She touched his clothes gently, almost lovingly.

Beyond was a lavish bathroom. A huge sunken tub, the size of a small pool, was made of bronze-veined marble. Rick's shaving things stood about on a matching marble counter. She breathed in the scent of his cologne, a subtle, yet heady fragrance.

She moved toward the bed. A heavy brown velvet quilt was carelessly tossed back, revealing beige and brown plaid sheets. She counted four pillows in a mound at one side of the bed. On that same side stood a massive night table, piled high with books and papers. The shade of the lamp had been removed. Apparently, Rick was a night reader. Michelle stared down at the slight imprint in the bed where earlier Rick had been lying. She trembled slightly.

Why was she doing this to herself? There was no going back on her decision. She was going to leave. And this was just making things more painful. Staring around the room, Rick's room, Michelle knew that there would never be a man in her life as powerful as Rick. No man could even come close. He dominated her thoughts. If he chose, he could bend her will to his.

She walked to the tall, rain-streaked windows. Her world was crashing around her.

Why did Rick McCord have to come back into her life? She had, after years of carefully disciplining herself, learned not to expect any special favors. And Rick was definitely a special favor. Before coming back to Harbor Springs, her memories of him had begun to dim a little. In time, she knew, they would have faded back into the recesses of her mind. But now, seeing him, living here with him for these few special days and weeks, all the old memories had sprung back into sharp focus. It would take a lifetime now to erase him from her mind. In fact, she didn't think a lifetime would be long enough. Without even trying, she could recall the smell of him, the roughness of his beard, the gruff tone he used when he was trying to control his temper.

Michelle hugged her arms tightly about herself and turned from the window. The sting of unshed tears burned her eyelids.

She crossed the room and stared at Rick's desk. It was littered with papers, blueprints, file folders. Did Rick ever escape from his work, she wondered, or did he take it with him wherever he went?

He would soon leave this place, his work here

finished. She knew how disciplined he was. He would be able to walk away from here without regrets. He would simply close this chapter of his life. She would be shut out of his thoughts as effectively as he had shut her out the other day in his garage. Rick would move on to a new project—a fresh challenge.

Michelle moved slowly around the room for a final, lingering glimpse of Rick's private life.

In his bathroom she picked up his shaver. Catching sight of her reflection in the mirror above the sink, she halted, startled. Her eyes were bloodshot from lack of sleep. Dark circles ringed her eyes. Her skin had lost its glow. She was pale, almost ashen. Wanting no further reminder of Rick's effect on her, she turned away.

In his dressing-room closet she halted and touched the sleeve of the suede jacket he had worn that first evening. He had seemed so aloof.

At the far corner of the closet hung a bulky, dust-covered storage bag. On an impulse, Michelle slid open the zipper, revealing an assortment of tweeds and velvets. Fingering a velvet smoking jacket, Michelle suddenly smiled. He was definitely not the tweed and velvet type. He was more the wool, suede and corduroy type, she thought, as an unbidden picture of Rick leaped into her mind.

These clothes must have belonged to Old Jacob Winter. Trang must have found them here and moved them aside for disposal later. As she stooped to rezip the storage bag, she noticed a bundle on the cardboard bottom. When she picked it up, she saw that it contained letters and papers tied together by a blue ribbon.

Kneeling on the floor, Michelle untied the ribbon and opened the first folded paper. A worn photograph dropped out. It showed a prim little girl with long fair ringlets, wearing riding jodhpurs and sitting astride a pony. The folded paper was a letter, written in a childish scrawl.

Dearest, darling Grandpa,

 Uncle Edward took this picture of me on their pony. Aunt Elizabeth sends her love. I want to come home.

All my love and kisses,
Marla.

Michelle stared for long moments at the photograph. Then she considered the packet of letters in her hands. She had no right to read them. Yet she knew she must. These two people, who had stirred her imagination when she was a little girl, were as real and significant as her own family had been. They had formed a part of her childhood. Though she had no right to intrude on their privacy, she couldn't stop herself.

Judging from the dates, Jacob Winter must have saved every letter Marla had ever written him. Some, undated, were the scribbling of a very young child, others revealed a precise handwriting of a young woman.

She opened another letter. She examined the enclosed photograph. Marla, radiant in a long gown, stood pressed against a tall, darkly handsome man. The look on the man's face was both proud and possessive. Marla was looking away from him, toward the camera. Michelle read the letter carefully:

Grandfather,

This is Enzo. His full name is Count Marius Enzo Benizetti III. I am flying home for Christmas. Enzo will be coming with me. We both want to talk to you.

Love, love, love.

Michelle studied the man in the photograph. He was truly handsome. No wonder Marla had been swept off her feet! A spoiled and inexperienced girl, she had impetuously followed her heart. She had ruthlessly overridden her grandfather's objections with the inevitable tragic results. But, at least, she had married her love! Even if briefly, she had known the joy of being married to the man she loved. Michelle sighed involuntarily as she picked up another letter.

She had lost all track of time, sitting on the floor in front of the closet, reading page after page of Marla's letters and poring over the old photographs, all carefully wrapped up in the appropriate letters. No matter how strongly old Jacob Winter had disapproved of his granddaughter's marriage, he had treasured all her letters.

A brief letter caused Michelle to gasp in shock.

Grandfather,

    You have your wish. Enzo has left. Gone back, I hear, to Lucia. I loved him.

Marla

Now there were no more letters for Michelle to peruse. Marla had been too proud to write. She had stubbornly refused to make up with the old man who had so resolutely refused to give his blessing to her ill-fated marriage. But he had kept her in his heart. Numerous newspaper clippings of Marla in Monaco, Marla in Paris, Marla in London fluttered through Michelle's fingers. But no more letters until the fat one at the bottom of the packet. Michelle opened it with trepidation. She remembered what Rick had told her of the tragic end of Jacob Winter's beautiful, beloved granddaughter who had so long ago filled his house with music and laughter.

Michelle pulled the creased, air-mail stationery from its torn envelope. Though the writing was obviously Marla's, it was not the precise, small script of her earlier years. Uneven characters sprawled across the thin pages. Here and there were blotches of ink? Tears? Michelle could not have told as she read through misty eyes Marla's last letter to her grandfather.

Dearest, darling Grandpa,

How long has it been since I called you that? Too long, I know. The bottom has fallen out of my world. So much I could never tell you. When Enzo left me, I was carrying his child. The pain of his leaving me was too much. I lost the baby. I'm afraid the past years have been lost in a blur. I am being released from the hospital tomorrow. I have been here for the past three months. Drying out. Now that I have faced up to what I have become, I must also face up to what I can do in the future. Grandfather, I want to come home. I know I must have caused great pain. I hope there is some way I can make it up to you. I cannot wait for your reply. Expect me within a few days.

All my love,
Marla.

Michelle stared at the letter in her hand. So, Marla had made peace with herself and her grandfather. Then she glanced at the last paper in the packet. It was a death certificate. It bore the name Jacob Winter. Michelle studied the date on the certificate. Then, she picked up Marla's last letter. The dates were the same. Jacob Winter had not lived long enough to receive this last letter, proclaiming his granddaughter's love, begging his foregiveness.

Michelle could imagine Marla Winter, exhausted, worn out, arriving home, hoping to find a loving, forgiving grandfather. Instead, she found only emptiness and guilt. She must have found the bundle of letters and photographs that her grandfather had saved through the years.

Michelle put the letter down with the others. She straightened the pile of papers and retied them with the faded, blue ribbon. She set the bundle in the bottom of the old storage bag. It represented the sum total of Marla Winter's love for her grandfather. And his for her. But it had been too late. Marla had waited too long to tell him what had always been in her heart.

Michelle walked slowly from Rick's room, swallowing the lump in her throat. It wouldn't take her long to pack. She hadn't brought that much with her.

When she had snapped her suitcase shut, she placed it by the foot of the bed and walked over to the window. It was covered with ice. If the temperature continued to drop, she might have to be here for days. Frowning, she gave a last look around the room, then went downstairs.

As she passed the library, Michelle was startled to see Rick at his desk. She had not heard him return, while she was upstairs packing.

Avoiding him, she headed for the kitchen. She settled down glumly at the table with a warming cup of tea. While she sipped her tea, she thought again about Marla and Jacob Winter. What a waste of years. All the things they should have said to each other. He, saving letters and clippings in the hope of keeping her close. She, still craving his approval even after breaking his heart. Michelle shook her head. All the barriers they erected. All those years wasted, when they could have brought so much love and joy to each other.

Michelle thought about that last futile letter. *Too late.* She sighed. *Poor Marla. Your letter was too late.*

Letter! The word drummed in her mind. Letter! Rick's voice shouting something about a letter. She had to think. What had he said? She had been in such a turmoil, his words hadn't really penetrated her conscience until now. She reeled as the impact of his words hit her.

"It doesn't matter now," Rick had said curtly. *"Nothing matters anymore. When you didn't even have the decency to answer my letters,* I knew you couldn't find it in your heart to forgive me for what my father did. I have no right to question the things you did to survive."

Michelle's hand flew to her mouth. *Letters!* Rick had written her *letters!* She flew down the hall and stopped in the doorway of the library.

Out of breath, she nearly choked on the words. "What *letters,* Rick?"

Rick's head shot up in surprise. "What? What are you shouting about, Mike?"

"I said, what *letters,* Rick? You mentioned *letters* you wrote me."

"Don't play any more games with me, Mike. I've had it with all the lies between us. You know very well what letters."

He stood up as she shouted, "I'm telling you the truth, Rick. I never received any letters."

He crossed the room in quick strides and clasped his hands tightly over her wrists. His face was grim, his mouth a thin, tight line of white anger. He was gripping her wrists so tightly she cried out in pain. Rick stared into her eyes, round with fear and surprise. Then, roughly, he released her and moved away from her. Michelle could feel the warmth leave her skin. He could warm her or chill her at will. He crossed to the fireplace and stared into the flames. A log smoked, then caught fire.

Rick turned and regarded her warily. "Did you know that your father came to see me the night—the last night we were together?"

Michelle nodded.

Rick turned back to the fire. "He was like a wild man. After what your sister Connie told him, I can't say I blamed him. I assured him over and over that nothing had happened. When he finally calmed down, he made me promise I wouldn't see you again. And I was not to attempt to contact you in any way."

Rick looked at the quiet figure across the room, holding herself rigidly erect. "Your father was right, Mike. You were so young, so vulnerable. He wanted you to have your chance at college first. He wanted you to taste life a little, before becoming—tied down. He told me it was in your best interest. He made me see that if I really cared for you, I would want what was best for you. I agreed. I gave him my word. We shook hands."

Rick distractedly ran his hand through his thick hair. "I figured you'd be hurt for a little while. Then you'd go off to college and forget all about me. Maybe I even believed I would be able to forget you too. I don't know anymore what I was thinking about. Anyway, Mike, I left town two days later." His features grew harsh, stiff, as he continued. "My father never said one word about what he knew about your father. He let me leave town not knowing what he planned. I was in Texas before I read about the scandal. I was as stunned by it all as I'm sure you were."

Rick caught Michelle's hand and pulled her nearer the fire. She shivered at the contact with his hand. She didn't want to face him. This was too painful.

Rick caught her chin in his hand and turned her face to his. "Mike. I knew how much you loved your father. I knew the publicity about your father's trouble must have been tearing you apart. I decided that I had a right to break my promise to your father. I phoned The Oaks here in Harbor Springs. You and your mother and Connie had already left. I tried your home in Detroit. No one would give me any information. So I wrote you a letter explaining everything. Then, a few days later, when I heard about your father's death . . ."

Michelle covered her face with her hands. She felt Rick's sudden movement away from her. Weakly, she leaned against a table.

"Mike, I telephoned. I wrote. I knew what you must be going through. But I never got through to you. Then, I wrote, asking if I could come to pay my respects to you and your family. I wanted to be sure first that my presence wouldn't offend anyone. Again, no reply. Finally, in desperation, I sat down and wrote you a long, rambling letter. Mike, like a love-sick fool, I poured out my heart to you. I told you all the things I couldn't say to you on that last night together."

His voice thickened. "That night, in the rose arbor . . ."

Michelle felt her face flame in humiliation. She still shuddered at Rick's rejection of her that night.

"My God, Mike! How I wanted you! But you were like some little child-woman. You were so innocent —so sheltered. I couldn't spoil our love like that." He turned bleak eyes on her. "I know I was rough on you that night, Mike. I handled it badly. But if I had been gentle with you, I wouldn't have been able to control myself. Don't you see, I had to be rough on you!"

Michelle nodded slowly, finally beginning to understand his actions on that night so long ago.

Rick said, "In my letter, I told you how much I loved and wanted you. I said that although I didn't know what was in store for me in the future, I wanted you to share my life with me. I begged you to let me come and take you back to Texas with me. I warned you that we wouldn't be living the kind of life we had known before. There weren't any yacht club races or country club dances. I knew that it would probably mean you would have to turn your back on anyone in your family who hated me for what my father did. But I needed you there at my side. And I believed that my love for you was so strong that it would make up for all the luxuries you'd have to give up."

He gazed at her tenderly. "I had no way of knowing your disastrous financial affairs, Mike. I just assumed that your father would have set aside something for your future. I guess he never dreamed he'd be caught. He probably thought he would be able to cover his tracks well enough to stay on top."

Michelle felt the sting of hot tears pricking her eyelids. She thought of the lean years she had faced alone. Years she could have shared with Rick.

Rick added, "And then in my letter, I begged you not to blame me for what my father had done to your father. I knew I was taking a chance on that. You had no way of knowing if I was telling you the truth when I claimed that I hadn't been aware of that whole ugly mess between our fathers. But, Mike, I really believed that if you loved me half as much as I loved you, there was no possible way you could blame me. I was so blinded by my love for you, I guess I stupidly believed that we could overcome any obstacle, even the mess our families had created."

He clenched his fists tightly at his side. "And I ended the letter by saying, 'Just pick up the phone and say one word. Yes.' That's all I needed to fly to your side and take you back with me."

Rick paced the floor like a caged animal. "I waited by that phone. I was so sure you would call. I loved you. I was convinced that would be enough. After several days, I phoned your house. Again, I couldn't get through to you. In desperation, I sent a telegram, asking if I could come. No reply. Nothing. It was a conspiracy of silence. And, Mike, I was certain that you were a part of that conspiracy."

Rick turned and stared at her bleakly. "And, finally, I said, 'What the hell!' I tore through life like a madman. I didn't bother to eat, forgot to sleep. I worked too hard." He laughed wryly. "I suppose you could say your rejection of me was the real reason I accomplished so much. I had so much excess energy to pour into my projects. I was determined to get over you, Mike, no matter what it took. I was sure I was the last person you ever wanted to see again."

Michelle crumpled weakly against the table. She thought of her mother, an invalid, alone in her bedroom every day while Michelle worked. When she found the job at Forest Corporation and dismissed all the servants, Michelle had made arrangements with a neighbor to come in and check on her mother each day. She could still picture Mrs. Emory, bringing the mail to her mother, making a pot of tea, sitting quietly and visiting each day while Michelle worked. The pile of mail would be spilled on her mother's night table, where Michelle would dutifully open it each evening and scan the bills. Often, her mother didn't even open letters of condolence. Michelle would have to read them aloud to her mother.

Michelle shook her head sadly. "Poor Mother. I didn't think she even glanced at the mail. I thought she had lost all interest in everything. Somehow, she must have decided to keep your letters and calls from me. I don't know why. I suppose she believed Connie's story, and thought she would save me from myself, or . . ." she glanced at Rick, "from your evil clutches. Whatever her reasons, I'm sure she thought she was doing the right thing. She took her secret to the grave."

Rick stood watching her. Finally he shook his head. "I really believed that you didn't love me enough or that you couldn't forgive me for what my father did."

"What your father did!" she cried. "It was my father who cheated and stole. Your father just exposed his crimes."

"Come on, Mike," he said in exasperation. "Don't try to be so noble. I know how much you loved your father. And my father destroyed him. I can imagine what that did to you."

Michelle looked up at Rick. She said, "When the accusations were first made public, I guess I thought your father was just trying to get even with my father for that ugly scene at your house. Connie had told me Dad went there. I was too stunned to think. But then, when I realized the truth, I believed that you had every right to avoid me. My father cheated your father out of a fortune, Rick."

As she lowered her eyes, Rick cupped her face in his hands and forced her to look at him. "I never blamed you, Mike." His thumbs traced the outline of her lips. His look softened. His eyes caressed her face. "I thought I could forget you in time. I traveled the whole world over to forget you," he said. "A million little things would remind me of you, Mike. I saw your eyes in the ocean, your hair in a flaming autumn leaf. I could never forget you. Heaven knows I tried."

His eyes lingered on her mouth. "And the day I heard about this house going on the market, I didn't even think. I just flew out and bought it. There was no dickering about price. I didn't care what it cost. I had to have this place. Foolishly, I thought it would bring you closer to me." He paused. "I'll always bless Jacob Winter and his granddaughter, Marla. Their house brought us together."

He frowned as he remembered. "After I bought this place, I became irrational. I flew to Detroit and spent an entire day going through the phone book. Don't ask me why. Maybe I thought I would just pick up the phone and tell you I was back. Something stupid like that. Of course, I was looking for Michelle Miller. Finally, I phoned a former neighbor of yours. She had heard that you married some young lawyer. She didn't know his name. That's when I threw in the towel. I flew back to my latest project and thought to hell with you."

A look of pain crossed his face momentarily, and he bent his head and whispered against her hair, "Mike. When you walked in this house with Jim Bannon, and he introduced you as Mrs. Scott, it was like someone had cut out my heart. I didn't think I could stand seeing you, working with you, and knowing you belonged to someone else."

"Then why did you arrange to keep me here?" she asked in surprise.

"I'm not sure what I wanted. I guess I thought I

would impress you with my success. No." He shook his head, causing the dark hair to fall slightly across his forehead. Michelle reached up to brush it away, and he caught her hand in midair and stopped her.

"No. I wasn't thinking at all. Just reacting. Now that I had found you again, I couldn't stand to let you go. I didn't know what I was going to do, but I had to go on seeing you. Even though it was torture to be near you and not be able to hold you. Mike!"

He reached out to hold her, but she backed away from his arms.

Michelle stared dazedly at Rick, his features still a grim mask from fatigue and anxiety. She dropped her hands limply to her sides in a gesture of resignation.

"I want you to know about David Scott," she said.

"No!" he shot back angrily. He reached out, roughly pulling her into his arms. She held herself stiffly away.

"I don't care whether you want to hear it or not. I intend to tell you," she said calmly.

She looked at the hard, tight line of his mouth. His black eyes narrowed as he watched her. She turned suddenly and stared out at the bleak scenery. A gust of wind shook the tree outside the window, sending a shower of red and gold and brown leaves to the ground. The tree stood naked, shivering in the wind. She drew her arms about herself and shivered.

Without turning around she began.

"I met David when I went back to Detroit, after the—trouble with my father. David was a clerk in Burt Matheson's law office. I didn't really notice him at first. He was very quiet, very . . ." She fumbled for the correct word. "He was . . . humble, sweet. When I would stop by Burt's office, it was usually David who would be sent for files or missing papers. Once in a while, Burt would send David to my place with papers he wanted me to sign. You have to understand, Rick. My father's estate was left in quite a tangle. He owned extensive properties and stocks. Burt had to untangle the mess—decide which ones we could sell, which titles were under a cloud. If it hadn't been for Burt's patience, I don't know how we would have survived those early months."

Michelle turned and glanced at Rick. His fists were clenched by his sides, and his face looked bleak. She turned back to the window and continued: "David was just there in the background, quiet and comforting. Sometimes, when he dropped off some papers at the house, I would invite him to stay and share dinner. Mother never left her bed by then, and the house was lonely. I learned a lot about David. He told me about his childhood. He was an orphan who had been shunted from one foster home to another. At sixteen, he ran away from an especially brutal foster father. He was taken before the juvenile authorities for a hearing. The court assigned him legal counsel. The lawyer befriended David, and before long he had David completely turned around. That lawyer, as I'm sure you've already guessed, was Burt Matheson. David began to study, and after graduation Burt persuaded David to try for college. Though not an especially good student, he managed to graduate with a decent average, and then applied to law school. It took him years to complete his courses. At one time, he carried three different jobs to finance his education. By the time I had met David, he was preparing for his bar exams and clerking in Burt's office. Burt was really fond of David. I think perhaps David became the son Burt and Anna never had."

Michelle moved into a path of sunlight, hugging her arms about herself for warmth.

"After Mother died, I sold the big house and moved to a small apartment. I sent Connie her share of the sale. She had taken off for California after she graduated from college. She didn't feel she had any reason to come back to Detroit."

Rick made a strangled gasp of disgust, but Michelle silenced him with a wave of her hand. "It doesn't matter anymore, Rick. Don't waste your anger on Connie. She was just afraid. I've forgiven her long ago," she added quietly.

"By then I was working days at Forest Corporation and going to college in the evenings. My days were so busy it came as a shock to realize one day that I hadn't seen David for a long time. I stopped by Burt's office to see what was happening. Burt explained that David was in the hospital. They didn't know what was wrong with him. Extreme fatigue. They were running some tests on him. So I started visiting David whenever I had a little time. He was in a ward with five other beds. He was in good spirits, and all of the men in the room cheered each other up. It was winter, and we were making plans for Christmas."

Michelle shivered suddenly and drew her arms tighter about her. She felt so cold, thinking about David. A bone-chilling cold that the heat of the room couldn't dispel. She turned to glance once more at Rick. He hadn't moved. He was staring transfixed at her.

"One day, when I dropped by the hospital, David was so depressed he could hardly speak. The tests were concluded. The diagnosis was leukemia. Advanced. They offered him no hope. I sat, holding his cold hand, staring at his pale face. He had turned into himself. I couldn't rouse him"

Michelle pressed her hands to her temples, as if to squeeze out the pain. Rick made a movement, as though to go to her, then stopped himself.

She went on. "When I left him that one day at the hospital, he was withdrawn, turned away from everyone. Just staring at the drab wall. There was nothing I could do for him. Then, the next afternoon, I stopped by on my way to class. He was still quiet, depressed. I suggested the doctors give him something to help him through this time. But then he started talking, and I realized why he was so low."

"David said, 'I've been lying here wondering why I drove myself so hard to get where I got, and then have to face the cold fact that it was all for nothing. Nothing! Do you know what bothers me most about dying like this?' he asked me. 'The fact that I have no one. No one to grieve for me. No one to remember me when I'm gone. No one to carry on my name.' Then he took my hands in his. He was squeezing them so tightly I almost cried out. 'Michelle,' he pleaded, 'if you married me now, right now, I'd have someone I know would love me when I died. Someone to grieve for me. Someone there to bury me. To care.' I caught my breath. How could I marry him? I was fond of David. He had been very kind to me during my difficult days. He was a comfort to me. But marry him? Love him? Cherish his memory? I promised him that I would think about it. I agonized over it for the entire night. By the next day, I knew what my answer would be. There was no way I could refuse. I spoke with his doctor. There was no question that David would never leave that hospital bed. And there was very little time left. So, I spoke with Burt and Anna. They agreed to be our witnesses. The minister came to the hospital that weekend. We were married there in the ward. David was too weak to stand. He lay in his bed. I stood beside him. He lived almost a week more. I was there each day after work. When he died, I was at his side. He had asked only that I arrange a simple funeral, and that I treasure his memory."

Michelle's voice came out in a choked rasp, almost a whisper. "David Scott was the kindest, bravest man I ever knew. And I did love him. Truly I did. I loved him in a very special way, Rick, and I always will."

As she turned toward him, crystal tears glittered in her blue-green eyes. She blinked, causing the tears to spill over her lower lids and trickle down her cheeks. Her lips quivered, but she refused to give in to the spasms of sobs which caught in her throat.

"Rick, you accused me of falling into the first pair of arms that were offered. Long before I married David, I had become resigned to the fact that you and I would never be together." She smiled grimly. "You were just a wonderful memory from happier days—schoolgirl days, where my biggest decisions were what movie to see, what clothes to wear. And I had put those days behind me, stored in the back of my mind. Reality was figuring out how to survive. Reality was facing David's death. Reality was knowing I would always be alone. Because you had spoiled it for anyone else. And I was convinced that you still blamed me for my father's crimes.

"Oh, Rick," she cried, "we kept all our feelings hidden behind masks. I really thought you couldn't stand the sight of me. I thought you just wanted to hurt me!"

Rick was across the room in swift strides. He gathered her into his arms and held her tightly against his chest. She stood rigid for several seconds, then seemed to crumple against him.

"Mike. Oh, Mike. Go on, my darling. Cry all you want. Oh, Mike," he crooned, as he held her tightly in his arms.

She finally gave in, crying as though her heart would break.

He held her tightly in his arms, feeling her body tremble as she tried to control the sobs.

Rick pressed his lips to her hair and murmured,

"For a tough little tomboy, you sure cry a lot. I seem to be always kissing away your tears."

She raised her head, and her lips trembled in a halting smile.

"You're shivering," he said gruffly. "Let's move nearer the fire."

Flames danced behind the closed screens of the fireplace.

"As long as you hold me, I'll be warm," she murmured.

Rick put his hands on her shoulders and stared down into her upturned face. "Mike. Since you first walked back into my life, it's been eating away at me that you belonged to someone else."

"Oh, Rick," Michelle said softly, "I was never really sure of that. You never admitted it. And you seemed so aloof. I was too proud to tell you that I was free and then have you say that you didn't want me. I had to go on with the lie. It was my only defense against your charm."

Rick tipped her head back with his thumb and finger under her chin. "Mike, after I plotted to keep you here, my scheme nearly destroyed me. Do you know how hard it was for me to get any work done with you here?" As she began to smile, he said harshly, "And you'll never know how close I came to just storming into your room late at night and forcing myself on you. Mike!" he groaned. "This whole thing has been tearing me apart."

"You!" she said, wrapping her arms around his waist. "How do you think I felt, living here with you and believing that you had never forgiven me for my father's crimes? I had to do everything necessary to keep you at a distance."

"Mike!" he growled fiercely. "No more misunderstandings! No more games. I love you more than anything in the world. I always have, since that first time I saw you, mad as a wet hen, floundering around in the lake. "

With his hands cupping both sides of her face, he said gruffly, "Promise me you'll marry me."

"Oh, Rick. I do love you. I'll always love you," she whispered.

"Then we'll start fresh," he murmured. "There are no barriers between us."

His fingers traced her eyebrows, down her cheek and across her lips. She felt the exquisite pain of waiting for the slow descent of his lips on hers. Standing on tiptoe, she spread her hands across his chest, then drew her arms slowly up to encircle his neck. Her fingers tangled in the thick dark hair curling at his neck. The warmth of their love spread through her limbs, leaving her clinging weakly to him. A familiar ache of desire began burning deep inside her, glazing her eyes.

Rick pressed his lips in her hair, and murmured in mock seriousness, "There's one problem, though, Mike."

"Ummm," she muttered. "You just promised me no barriers." She kissed the corner of his mouth. "So, what's the problem? "

"I'm afraid you're going to have to share your kitchen with an overbearing Vietnamese houseman," he whispered against her temple.

"Considering his temper and mine, I'm sure the sparks will fly every once in a while," she said, smiling. "But I'm willing to put up with it as long as you don't replace Mac with a beautiful female secretary."

"Don't worry," he whispered as he pulled her roughly against him. "You're going to be all the beautiful woman I can handle, and this time there will be no Connie to interrupt us—"

"Is that a threat or a promise, Mr. McCord?" Michelle murmured before Rick's deep kiss had stopped her smiling lips.

Silhouette Romance

IT'S YOUR OWN SPECIAL TIME

Contemporary romances for today's women.
Each month, six very special love stories will be yours
from SILHOUETTE. Look for them wherever books are sold
or order now from the coupon below.

$1.50 each

___# 1 PAYMENT IN FULL Hampson

___# 2 SHADOW AND SUN Carroll

___# 3 AFFAIRS OF THE HEART Powers

___# 4 STORMY MASQUERADE Hampson

___# 5 PATH OF DESIRE Goforth

___# 6 GOLDEN TIDE Stanford

___# 7 MIDSUMMER BRIDE Lewis

___# 8 CAPTIVE HEART Beckman

___# 9 WHERE MOUNTAINS WAIT Wilson

___#10 BRIDGE OF LOVE Caine

___#11 AWAKEN THE HEART Vernon

___#12 UNREASONABLE SUMMER Browning

___#13 PLAYING FOR KEEPS Hastings

___#14 RED, RED ROSE Oliver

___#15 SEA GYPSY Michaels

___#16 SECOND TOMORROW Hampson

___#17 TORMENTING FLAME John

___#18 THE LION'S SHADOW Hunter

___#19 THE HEART NEVER FORGETS Thornton

___#20 ISLAND DESTINY Fulford

___#21 SPRING FIRES Richards

___#22 MEXICAN NIGHTS Stephens

___#23 BEWITCHING GRACE Edwards

___#24 SUMMER STORM Healy

___#25 SHADOW OF LOVE Stanford

___#26 INNOCENT FIRE Hastings

___#27 THE DAWN STEALS SOFTLY Hampson

___#28 MAN OF THE OUTBACK Hampson

___#29 RAIN LADY Wildman

___#30 RETURN ENGAGEMENT Dixon

___#31 TEMPORARY BRIDE Halldorson

___#32 GOLDEN LASSO Michaels

___#33 A DIFFERENT DREAM Vitek

___#34 THE SPANISH HOUSE John

___#35 STORM'S END Stanford

___#36 BRIDAL TRAP McKay

___#37 THE BEACHCOMBER Beckman

___#38 TUMBLED WALL Browning

___#39 PARADISE ISLAND Sinclair

___#40 WHERE EAGLES NEST Hampson

___#41 THE SANDS OF TIME Owen

___#42 DESIGN FOR LOVE Powers

___#43 SURRENDER IN PARADISE Robb

___#44 DESERT FIRE Hastings

___#45 TOO SWIFT THE MORNING Carroll

___#46 NO TRESPASSING Stanford

___#47 SHOWERS OF SUNLIGHT Vitek

___#48 A RACE FOR LOVE Wildman

___#49 DANCER IN THE SHADOWS Wisdom

___#50 DUSKY ROSE Scott

___#51 BRIDE OF THE SUN Hunter

___#52 MAN WITHOUT A HEART Hampson

___#53 CHANCE TOMORROW Browning

___#54 LOUISIANA LADY Beckman

___#55 WINTER'S HEART Ladame

___#56 RISING STAR Trent

___#57 TO TRUST TOMORROW John

___#58 LONG WINTER'S NIGHT Stanford

___#59 KISSED BY MOONLIGHT Vernon

___#60 GREEN PARADISE Hill

___ #61 WHISPER MY NAME Michaels
___ #62 STAND-IN BRIDE Halston
___ #63 SNOWFLAKES IN THE SUN Brent
___ #64 SHADOW OF APOLLO Hampson
___ #65 A TOUCH OF MAGIC Hunter
___ #66 PROMISES FROM THE PAST Vitek
___ #67 ISLAND CONQUEST Hastings
___ #68 THE MARRIAGE BARGAIN Scott
___ #69 WEST OF THE MOON St. George
___ #70 MADE FOR EACH OTHER Afton Bonds
___ #71 A SECOND CHANCE ON LOVE Ripy
___ #72 ANGRY LOVER Beckman
___ #73 WREN OF PARADISE Browning
___ #74 WINTER DREAMS Trent
___ #75 DIVIDE THE WIND Carroll
___ #76 BURNING MEMORIES Hardy
___ #77 SECRET MARRIAGE Cork
___ #78 DOUBLE OR NOTHING Oliver
___ #79 TO START AGAIN Halldorson

___ #80 WONDER AND WILD DESIRE Stephens
___ #81 IRISH THOROUGHBRED Roberts
___ #82 THE HOSTAGE BRIDE Dailey
___ #83 LOVE LEGACY Halston
___ #84 VEIL OF GOLD Vitek
___ #85 OUTBACK SUMMER John
___ #86 THE MOTH AND THE FLAME Adams
___ #87 BEYOND TOMORROW Michaels
___ #88 AND THEN CAME DAWN Stanford
___ #89 A PASSIONATE BUSINESS James
___ #90 WILD LADY Major
___ #91 WRITTEN IN THE STARS Hunter
___ #92 DESERT DEVIL McKay
___ #93 EAST OF TODAY Browning
___ #94 ENCHANTMENT Hampson
___ #95 FOURTEEN KARAT BEAUTY Wisdom
___ #96 LOVE'S TREACHEROUS JOURNEY Beckman
___ #97 WANDERER'S DREAM Clay
___ #98 MIDNIGHT WINE St. George
___ #99 TO HAVE, TO HOLD Camp

$1.75 each

___ # 100 YESTERDAY'S SHADOW Stanford
___ # 101 PLAYING WITH FIRE Hardy
___ # 102 WINNER TAKE ALL Hastings
___ # 103 BY HONOUR BOUND Cork
___ # 104 WHERE THE HEART IS Vitek
___ # 105 MISTAKEN IDENTITY Eden
___ # 106 THE LANCASTER MEN Dailey
___ # 107 TEARS OF MORNING Bright
___ # 108 FASCINATION Hampson
___ # 109 FIRE UNDER SNOW Vernon
___ # 110 A STRANGER'S WIFE Trent
___ # 111 WAYWARD LOVER South

___ # 112 WHISPER WIND Stanford
___ # 113 WINTER BLOSSOM Browning
___ # 114 PAINT ME RAINBOWS Michaels
___ # 115 A MAN FOR ALWAYS John
___ # 116 AGAINST THE WIND Lindley
___ # 117 MANHATTAN MASQUERADE Scott
___ # 118 FOR THE LOVE OF GOD Dailey
___ # 119 DESIRE Hampson
___ # 120 TAKE THIS LOVE Carroll
___ # 121 JUST LIKE YESTERDAY Langan
___ # 122 WINTERFIRE Scofield
___ # 123 HOLIDAY IN JAMAICA Sinclair

Silhouette *Romance*

15-Day Free Trial Offer
6 Silhouette Romances

6 Silhouette Romances, free for 15 days! We'll send you 6 new Silhouette Romances to keep for 15 days, absolutely free! If you decide not to keep them, send them back to us. You pay nothing.

Free Home Delivery. But if you enjoy them as much as we think you will, keep them by paying the invoice enclosed with your free trial shipment. We'll pay all shipping and handling charges. You get the convenience of Home Delivery and we pay the postage and handling charge each month.

Don't miss a copy. The Silhouette Book Club is the way to make sure you'll be able to receive every new romance we publish before they're sold out. There is no minimum number of books to buy and you can cancel at any time.